"Get down!" Quinn hollered as a shot rang out, hitting the back of his truck's bed.

He grabbed hold of Dana and pushed her to the seat.

"Who are they?" she shouted.

Gripping the steering wheel, Quinn kicked in to survival mode, swerving on the road to make them more difficult to hit. He glanced out the mirror at the pursuing car and saw both the driver and passenger were wearing masks. "I wish I knew."

Another shot sounded, this one shattering the back window. Dana covered her head with her hands as she crouched by the seat as best she could.

A third shot hit the tire. Quinn heard the pop of the rubber blow, then the truck veered sharply to the right, sending them spinning. He turned into the spin, doing his best to right the vehicle, but the truck was going too fast.

"Hang on," he managed to shout before the truck smashed into the guardrail and tilted into the air. His seat belt locked as he was thrown forward, and he heard Dana scream as the truck plummeted down the embankment, rolling with each sickening second.

Virginia Vaughan is a born-and-raised Mississippi girl. She is blessed to come from a large Southern family, and her fondest memories include listening to stories recounted around the dinner table. She was a lover of books from a young age, devouring tales of romance, danger and love. She soon started writing them herself. You can connect with Virginia through her website, virginiavaughanonline.com, or through the publisher.

Books by Virginia Vaughan

Love Inspired Suspense

Covert Operatives

Cold Case Cover-Up

Rangers Under Fire

Yuletide Abduction
Reunion Mission
Ranch Refuge
Mistletoe Reunion Threat
Mission Undercover
Mission: Memory Recall

No Safe Haven

COLD CASE COVER-UP

VIRGINIA VAUGHAN

HARLEQUIN® LOVE INSPIRED® SUSPENSE

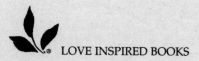

LOVE INSPIRED BOOKS

Recycling programs
for this product may
not exist in your area.

ISBN-13: 978-1-335-49057-5

Cold Case Cover-Up

Printed in U.S.A.

For I know the thoughts that I think toward you,
saith the Lord, thoughts of peace, and not of evil,
to give you an expected end.
–Jeremiah 29:11

To Jon Michael and Carter.
You've given my life new meaning. I love you.

ONE

Someone was watching her.

The hairs on her neck prickled a warning. Dana Lang glanced around the coffee shop but saw no one looking her way or appearing fixated on her. Still, her instincts were never wrong. As a television investigative journalist, she was used to people recognizing her, but this felt different. This felt like daggers in her back.

She tried to shake off the feeling and tell herself she was being silly. No one in this sleepy little town of West Bend, Missouri, knew her. She glanced at the television mounted to the wall while she waited for her coffee to be ready. The news channels were still reporting about the embassy attack six weeks earlier and the heroic eight-man team of CIA-contracted security operatives who'd rescued eighteen Americans trapped inside. Five people had died in all, including two of the operatives involved in the rescue.

She accepted her drink as her own interview with one of the contractors replayed in her mind. She'd stumbled upon a gold mine when Michael "Rizzo" Ricardo had contacted her wanting to tell his story about the night of the attack and how the US government had ordered the operatives to stand down. They'd defied orders instead and become national heroes in the process. He'd felt betrayed by his government's response to the attack and wanted to let the world know it. Until his interview, only the names of the two operatives who had died—Tommy Woods and Mike Piven—had been released.

Dana ignored the reminder that she needed to be back in Chicago—or anywhere but West Bend—digging in to Rizzo's life and trying to uncover the identities of his teammates to corroborate his story. So far, Rizzo was the only one to come forward to tell the tale of being abandoned by their country during the attack.

But she resisted the urge to pack up and leave. Every reporter in the nation was vying for that story, and while uncovering the names of the other operatives would be a monumental boost to her career, the case she was focusing on now would impact her life so much more. Five days ago, the night before her interview with Rizzo, she'd discovered a box in her late mother's belongings that had shattered her world and sent her on this quest to West Bend to uncover the truth about her lineage.

The box she'd found had contained adoption papers. Dana had never even known she'd been adopted. But the surprises hadn't ended there. She'd also discovered a newspaper article about the murders of Rene Renfield and her infant daughter, Alicia, along with a photograph that looked suspiciously like one of Dana's own baby photos. There was also a letter from the preacher who'd arranged her adoption that explained to her parents how she'd been left at the church, which had been considered a safe haven, by someone he trusted who'd insisted the child was in danger and needed to be believed dead. And there was a short note from the person who'd abandoned her. She didn't know if her parents had ever discovered anything solid in their questioning, if they'd taken the preacher's word and decided not to rock the boat, or if her father's death in a car wreck when Dana was eleven had ended their search for answers. Regardless, now that she knew, she was determined to finish their investigation and uncover the truth. Was she Alicia Renfield? And, if she was, who murdered her birth mother and left her for dead?

Dana exited the coffee shop and headed back to her hotel. As she walked, she noticed the stares and curious glances of the townspeople. She'd heard small towns were notorious for their gossip grapevines, but she'd only arrived yesterday. Did these people know she was here to investigate a thirty-year-old murder, or had they recognized her from her job as a TV cold case reporter on *Newswatch*? For all she knew, they could be staring because she was an unfamiliar face in a town where everybody knew everybody else.

But these stares didn't feel sinister, not like the one she'd felt in the coffee shop. Her friends had tried to warn her that she wouldn't be accepted into a small town as a stranger poking her nose into the town's business, but it was her business, too. This terrible crime had left West Bend in a state of shock, but it may have also forever changed her path. She'd try to confirm her suspicions, and if they were true, find out who killed her mother and why.

As she walked, she checked off her itinerary in her head. She'd already been to the local library and made friends with Lila, the librarian, who'd told her all their newspaper archives from thirty years earlier were still on microfiche. Their digital records only went back twenty years. Tomorrow, she would make a day of checking out the old newspaper articles on the murder. This evening, she was heading to the sheriff's office to have a closer look at the police files for the case. The records clerk, a lovely woman named Beverly Shorter, had been pleasant enough on the phone and offered to help her in any way possible, but when Dana had mentioned the Renfield murders, she'd insisted the records were not available for public access since it was still an open case. Dana was confident she could change Beverly's mind. She'd built a successful career by breaking news stories and you didn't do that by accepting *no* for an answer.

She stopped suddenly and turned, that prickling sensation rushing through her again. She glanced at the people on the street but saw nothing suspicious—no one was focusing excessively on her. But how would she even recognize something out of the ordinary here? She didn't know these people. And who would have a reason to follow her?

Her phone buzzed in her pocket. She pulled it out and checked the caller ID. It was her producer, Mason Sheffield. She sent the call to voice mail. She didn't want to talk to him right now. He'd agreed to give her this time off even though he wanted her on the embassy-bombing story and following up on Rizzo's colleagues. But as big as that story was, this one would impact her life forever. She'd interviewed countless families of victims of crime and listened to them talking about their loved ones and their longing to see justice done. She realized she wanted that, too. Besides, the Ricardo case was stalled until more members of the secret CIA security detail came forward or were outed as operatives. She knew there were other reporters following leads to their whereabouts, but she couldn't think about that now. This case, proving her identity and finding out who murdered her birth mother and who left her abandoned and alone as an infant, was her main focus now. She'd been alone for too long. It was time to discover who she was once and for all.

She walked into the hotel and nodded at the desk clerk who'd checked her in the previous evening. He was a humorous man and had recognized her from her show. Had he tipped off everyone in town that she was staying at his hotel? Could that explain her eerie feeling of being followed?

She got into the elevator and willed it to close before anyone jumped in with her. No one did and she breathed a sigh of relief when the doors slid shut. She rode it to the third floor then got off. Her room was at the end of the hall, but she stopped after only a few steps. The hairs on her neck stood on end again as she saw the door to her room was open. The elevator closed behind her and dinged, startling her. She took a deep breath to calm her racing heart. She could call hotel security or the police, but how silly would she feel if it was only housekeeping refreshing the towels? No, she was allowing her imagination to run wild and that sense of being watched to control her. Still, as she moved down the hallway, bracing to confront whoever was there, she wished she had something to defend herself with. Her iced coffee wasn't going to stop anyone. Why hadn't she ordered it hot? She inched toward the open doorway and heard noise coming from inside.

Someone was definitely in her room!

She pushed open the door and spotted a figure clad in black digging through her suitcase.

"Who are you?" she called.

The intruder turned her way, his face covered by a mask. Before she could move, he ran toward her, shouldered past her and knocked her backward into the wall. She screamed as she fell, her coffee spraying into the air. She pulled herself up in time to see the intruder burst through the door to the stairwell, then he was gone.

She quickly crawled to her feet, scooped up her cell phone and dialed 911. When the operator came on asking for her emergency, Dana replied, "Some-one broke into my hotel room."

"What's the address, ma'am?"

She walked into her room, ready to give the ad-dress of the hotel, when something else grabbed her attention. On the wall, she'd pinned up her notes about the case, the newspaper article she'd found in her mother's belongings, the letter from the preacher and the note left with her when she was abandoned as a baby. Plastered on the wall beneath that in big, black, spray-painted letters were the words *Go Home*.

"Ma'am, are you still there? I need to know where you are."

She rattled off the name of the hotel then, before hanging up, whispered, "Please hurry."

I'm not ready for this.

Quinn Dawson parked his cruiser in front of the hotel and got out. He was tired, emotionally and physically. He'd often moonlighted as a reserve dep-uty for his father whenever he wasn't on assignment overseas providing covert security for the CIA as part of the Security Operations Abroad, or SOA as they referred to the company, and his father thought doing so now would be good for him, but Quinn wasn't so sure. He was still reeling from the attack on the embassy and the grief of losing his best friend in the fight that ensued. He wasn't sure he was up for battling crime in his own hometown.

He entered the hotel lobby and was greeted by Milo Sherman, the night clerk, who handed him a room key and pointed to a woman sitting in a chair at one side of the small lobby. He sized her up as he headed her way. Even if she hadn't been staying in the hotel, he'd have known she wasn't a local because of the high-end heels she wore. And if he'd seen those long legs before, he would have remembered.

She sat with her head down and her long blond hair hanging over her face, but the sight of her when she glanced up at him nearly sent him falling backward and hightailing it out of the hotel. He checked that response and maintained his cool, recognizing her long thin face, soft brown eyes and the subtle curve of her lips.

Dana Lang.

He'd never met her before, but he knew her. She was the reporter who'd interviewed one of his teammates, Rizzo, and plastered his name and face all over the world. When a frenzied mob bent on destruction and murder had attacked an embassy compound in Libya six weeks ago, Quinn, Rizzo and the rest of their group had orchestrated a counterattack and rescued eighteen Americans. Unfortunately, five people had died in the incident, including two operatives, one of them Quinn's best friend, Tommy Woods. The encounter itself had stirred up a storm of controversy, reignited by Rizzo Ricardo's proclamation that he'd been there and participated in the rescue, and that his government had left them all to die. The press, led by Dana Lang, had jumped on his story and catapulted him to stardom in a matter of days. They'd also pressured him to name his other teammates. So far, Rizzo had held out, but Quinn suspected it was only a matter of time before his own name became associated with the incident as well. And being outed as a former Delta operator and current SOA member would not only put his life in danger, but could also end his career. Now, this reporter was here in his hometown. Had Rizzo given up his name already? He took in a sharp breath and braced himself for the barrage of questions he was certain was about to blast him.

However, when she stood and pulled back her hair, he saw the redness in her eyes and the way her hands shook as she held one out to him. Was it possible this wasn't a ploy to draw him here after all?

"Thank you for coming, Deputy. My name is—"

"Dana Lang. I know who you are."

She gave him a gracious smile he was certain she used for fans of her show. He'd never said he was a fan.

He nodded, deciding it was better not to draw attention to himself in case she hadn't yet realized who he was. She couldn't have known tonight was the night he'd finally conceded to his father's urgings and decided to work. "Can you tell me what happened?"

She nodded and took a deep breath, and as she began talking, he could see her hands quiver. She was shaken up. That couldn't be faked. "I was returning to my room when I noticed the door open. When I entered, someone was in there going through my belongings. I said something and he turned to look at me, then pushed past me and ran down the hall into the stairwell. He knocked me down as he fled." She motioned to her stained blouse. "That's how I spilled iced coffee all over me."

"Did you recognize him?"

"No, and I didn't get a good look at him. He was tall and thin, but his face was hidden by a ski mask. And when he ran toward me, I was too startled to really get a good look."

"What was missing from your room?"

"Nothing."

"He didn't take anything?" That surprised him. Most break-ins were burglaries. Had she interrupted him before he could find anything of value?

"Not that I can tell. My belongings were scattered, but I don't think anything was missing. I had my cell phone and wallet with me and I didn't bring anything valuable, so there wasn't much for him to take. But he did leave something. A threatening message spray-painted on the wall."

He jotted down notes, then asked her to follow him upstairs. Now that she had the benefit of time and someone else with her, perhaps she would notice something else that could help pinpoint who'd done this deed.

She walked with him to the elevator, her arms curled over her chest and her head low, and stepped inside with hesitation.

"No one's going to hurt you," he assured her. "I'm here with you." He touched her elbow, trying to re-assure her, but instantly regretted it as a spark raced up his hand. He had no business noticing how dainty and soft her arm was or breathing in the sweet scent of her shampoo. This woman could ruin his life with one story. He had to remain on his guard around her at all times.

He cleared his throat as he tried to regain his composure and act professionally. "How long have you been in town?"

"I arrived last night," she told him.

Welcome to West Bend, he thought, hating that this would forever be the image she'd take from his hometown.

The elevator doors slid open and she hesitated a moment before getting out, then let him take the lead as they walked down the hall.

He unlocked her door with the key Milo had given him and pushed it open. Clothes were scattered from a suitcase onto the bed. Drawers were open. Someone had been searching for something, and by the look of the room, he'd been here a while. If he hadn't stolen anything, it was either because he hadn't found anything of value, or else that wasn't the reason he'd come.

He turned and saw a display on the wall of photos and notes, along with the threatening graffiti Dana had mentioned. It looked like she was making an evidence board. He glanced at the date on an Associated Press article about a murder in his hometown and realized it was referencing the Renfield murders, a thirty-year-old cold case.

"Is this all for an upcoming show?" he asked her.

"Sort of. It's a case that's recently caught my interest. What do you know about the murders?"

He let his gaze fall back to the wall of what seemed to him random information. Was it possible this was the reason she was in town and it had nothing to do with him? *Please, God, please.* "Just what I've heard throughout the years. Rumors, gossip, folklore, that's all."

"Do you think he killed her? Paul Renfield? The article says he killed his wife and child. Do you think he did it?"

He shrugged. "That's what they say."

"Did they ever find him? I have the AP article that got picked up, but the local newspaper's files aren't online so I don't really know what happened after the initial report. I had planned on spending this evening digging into the files at the sheriff's office, but after this, I think I'll stay in tonight instead."

He remembered hearing about this case when he was a kid. His grandfather had been the sheriff at the time of the murders and Quinn knew the murder of that mother and little girl had haunted him until his dying day. It was a case he'd never been able to solve. "It was a long time ago."

He wasn't really in to having this conversation with her. All he wanted was to take her statement and get out before her radar zeroed in on him. It was too coincidental that she was in his town when Rizzo's story was splashed all over the news. "It was before my time. I didn't know any of these people so I can't really say."

But as he scanned the wall again, his gaze landed on one of the handwritten notes and he realized he recognized that writing. He pulled it from the wall and read the short missive.

Please take care of this child. She just became an orphan.

"What is it?" she asked him, suddenly alert and beside him, her face anxious with curiosity.

"It looks like my grandfather's handwriting. He was the sheriff back when the murders happened, so it's not odd to see his handwriting. I guess it caught me off guard." He pinned the paper back to the wall.

She stepped closer to him and glanced at the sheet of paper he'd held. "You recognize this handwriting as your grandfather's? Are you certain? And your grandfather was the sheriff at the time of murders? Sheriff Bill Mackey?"

"That's right. Why?"

"This note, the one with his handwriting, was left with a child at a church sixty miles from here just days after the murders took place. It was the only clue pointing to who left her, since the preacher didn't tell the adoptive parents."

He frowned. What was she talking about? "I've never heard that."

"Few people have." She locked eyes with him. They were now on fire with excitement. "I don't think Alicia Renfield died that night at all. I think she was found alive and your grandfather not only knew it, he hid her away and faked her death."

She was crazy. Or was she so hungry for a story that she would resort to making up nonsense? He shook his head and backed away from her, anger biting at him. His grandfather had been a hero in this town and to him. His death two years ago had rocked Quinn. Her accusations were unthinkable. He grimaced and locked eyes with her, his body now on alert. "Watch what you say about my grandfather. He was a good man. He would never be involved in what you're accusing him of."

"You said yourself the handwriting matched."

He grimaced, then tried to backtrack. "Maybe I was wrong. It could belong to anyone." He shouldered past her and started to walk out, but he stopped. She was back in town to investigate this murder and it seemed as if she intended to drag his grandfather's good name through the mud to get her story. "He was a good sheriff, and he was a good man."

"I'm trying to find out the truth about what happened that night."

"And you don't care who you hurt in the process, do you?"

Her eyes widened in surprise at his accusation. "I'm only trying to uncover the truth. My goal isn't to harm anyone."

"It doesn't matter that he's not here to defend himself anymore?"

She sighed. "Look, I'm not trying to say Sheriff Mackey committed the murders. I only want to find

out what he covered up and why. I have a letter from
the preacher of the church that says whoever left the
child with him believed she was in danger. He died
six years ago, so I can't question him. Besides, your
grandfather may be dead, but someone obviously
doesn't want me looking into this." She pointed at
the graffiti on the wall to confirm her words.

She was right. Someone had broken into her room.
And this wasn't a random burglary, either. Whoever
it was hadn't stolen anything, which meant they had
either been interrupted before finding what they were
looking for, or they just wanted to see what she was
investigating and what evidence she had. And they'd
come paint-in-hand to warn her off.

She jutted out her chin stubbornly, but he could
see the fear reflected in her brown eyes. "I'll admit
I was a little rattled by this, but I won't be scared
off so easily."

He shouldn't be allowing her to get under his skin,
but he found himself admiring the way she tried
to show him a strong front when she was so obviously frightened of what had happened here tonight.
It made him want to find who did this, but he knew
that was unlikely. "I'll make a report, but it's doubt-
ful we'll catch them. It won't do much good to run
prints since this is a hotel room and we wouldn't be
able to exclude anyone."

"I understand." She pulled at the collar of her
shirt, a nervous gesture that belied the calm she was
trying to show him. "Thank you for coming, Deputy…"

"Dawson," he said. "Quinn Dawson."

She arched an eyebrow. "Any relation to Sheriff Dawson?"

He nodded. She'd done her homework. "My father."

"I see. Law enforcement in this town must be a family matter."

"My brother, Rich, is also on the force full-time. I'm only a reserve deputy. I fill in whenever I'm in town."

"Oh, what do you do the rest of the time?"

He grimaced. Why had he said that? He strived to be as vague as possible with his response. The last thing he wanted was to direct her radar his way if she really wasn't on to him. "Private security." He put away his notebook and handed her a card with the sheriff department's information. "If you have any further issues or need any more information, call this number."

"Thank you. I've already spoken to Beverly in your records department. I'm hoping to get a look at the case file, but she assures me it's an open case and the records aren't available to the public. Any tips on getting her to change her mind?"

"Beverly won't release anything without my father's approval."

"How cooperative do you think your father will be about releasing that information?"

He knew. Zero cooperation. "I hope you have a plan B," he told her before walking out.

The next morning, Dana was met with opposition at the sheriff's office just as Quinn had predicted.

"The Renfield murders are still technically an

open case and we don't comment to the press on open cases." Sheriff John Dawson was sharp and clear in his tone. He apparently didn't care for Dana sticking her nose into his town's business and he wasn't going to help her do it.

She wondered if Quinn had told his father that she'd come to town to drag his grandfather's—Sheriff Dawson's father-in-law's—name through the mud. That wasn't her intention. She wished Quinn believed that, but then why did she care what he thought? The truth was she was touched by the way he'd stood up for his grandfather. He had a family here and he was looking out for them. She liked that. Her own family had disintegrated when her father was killed. Her mother had lost herself in her grief and work and had eventually sent Dana away to boarding school. They had never regained their connection before her mother's death last month, but Dana still remembered the times when they'd been a family. When she'd broken up with her boyfriend, Jason, several months ago, she was left wondering if she would ever have family of her own again. She'd been looking forward to marriage and one day soon having children. Jason had shattered those dreams when he'd run off with his physical therapist, and her mother's death had left her completely alone in the world.

She sighed. No use swooning over the ruggedly handsome Quinn Dawson. She imagined he was looking forward to one day having a wife and four or five kids and living the small-town family dream. She wasn't really suited for that kind of life. She glanced around the room at Rich Dawson. He'd already moved up in ranks and she figured he would one day follow in his father and grandfather's footsteps and become sheriff. Did Quinn have those same ambitions? By his own admission, he'd taken a job outside of his family's chosen profession. Was there some reason he hadn't climbed on board the law enforcement career train?

She felt herself flush. He was right about her. She was always questioning things. Asking too many questions and allowing her thought process to go off in a million different directions. But she was a reporter and that was her job.

She locked eyes with Sheriff Dawson. "Is this case being actively investigated?"

"Not at this time. It's been a while since we've had any leads."

"Can you tell me when it was last actively investigated."

He stood, promptly ending the conversation. "I appreciate your position, but as I said, we don't release information on open cases."

It wasn't the first time she'd gotten flak from local authorities not wanting to share their records, but she was a little surprised that she wasn't able to convince Sheriff Dawson to change his mind. Her charm and notoriety almost always worked.

"Sheriff, the case is thirty years old. Surely, you can make an exception given the age of the investigation. This may very well be a case where fresh eyes can make a difference."

"My father-in-law was the sheriff at the time of these murders. I was friends with Paul and Rene Renfield. This town was shaken to its core by this incident. Believe me, Miss Lang, the case has been thoroughly investigated. Two people died that night, a woman and child, but this entire town was affected by it."

She stood, too, realizing she wasn't going to get anywhere with him. He wasn't open to fresh eyes. But how would he feel if she presented him with evidence that Alicia Renfield didn't die that night after all? Would he even believe the note had been written in his own father-in-law's hand?

She thanked him, then walked out of his office without mentioning the note. If Quinn wanted to tell him, then so be it, but she wasn't going to share her information if they weren't willing to do the same.

Quinn heard the commotion in his dad's office when he entered the deputies' bullpen. All eyes were on the scene going on inside that office. From the best he could see, Dana Lang was standing up to his father without fear or hesitation. It took a strong person not to be intimidated by his angry glare. John Dawson had certainly been elected as sheriff based on his name and family connections because his curt personality left something to be desired. Quinn turned his gaze to his brother. Rich would be a successful sheriff one day. He had both the investigative skills and the personality to win people over, as well as a wife and kids everyone in town loved. He also had good ideas for the department, but first he had to wait out his father's retirement or election defeat by another opponent, neither of which seemed would happen anytime soon.

The door opened and Dana walked out. Quinn set down his coffee as she headed his way, waving and flashing him a grateful smile. "Good morning. Well, you were right. He wouldn't release them."

He gave an easy shrug, noticing how much more put together she seemed today. The coffee stains were gone and her hair and makeup were perfect, but he didn't miss the puffiness that remained around her eyes—evidence of her ordeal. She was certainly beautiful but he liked her more relaxed look from last night. This morning, she could have just stepped out of the hair-and-makeup department of her television show. "Can't say I'm surprised. How was everything last night? Any other incidents?"

"None. Milo offered to transfer me to another room and I took him up on it. I don't think I would have been able to sleep with those words glaring down on me all night."

"I'm glad Milo took care of you."

"How about you? Anything else exciting happen in town last night?"

He gave a slow shake of his head. His shifts were usually free from a lot of drama, but last night had been a snooze fest after he'd left her. "Nope, nothing. Besides your incident, it was all quiet everywhere else, too."

"Good, that's good. Well, it was nice to see you

again, Quinn. I'd better be going. I have an appoint-
ment at the library with a microfiche machine."

"You take care, Miss Lang. And be careful. Whoever wrote that threat knows what case you're working on and obviously doesn't like it."

She gave him a smile, but he could see she didn't
need to be reminded that someone had targeted her.
She'd probably spent most of the night unable to
sleep from listening to noises outside and worry-
ing that whoever had broken into her room would
return with more than a paint can. "Thanks for the
concern, but I'll be fine. It's not the first time someone has tried to convince me to stop investigating.
I'll be careful, though. And, please, call me Dana."

He watched her walk out and realized he admired
her tenacity. She was a tough lady and was determined to see this case through. He knew his grandfather wasn't involved in the murders, but the image
of that note kept running through his mind. If he'd
written it, then he had been complicit in abandoning a child and possibly faking her death. Quinn had
nearly convinced himself that he'd been wrong about
the handwriting and it wasn't his grandfather's, but
he'd been so sure when he'd first seen it.

"What are you doing here, Quinn?" Rich asked,
coming up behind him, his voice holding a tinge of
irritation. Quinn already knew the reason his brother
was on edge. She was walking out the door. "Do you
have any idea who that woman is?"

Quinn scrubbed a hand through his hair. "I know.
I recognized her. Dana Lang. I got called in last night

for a break-in at her hotel room. She says she's working on a story about the Renfield murders."

Rich was one of the few people who knew about
Quinn's involvement in the embassy attack. He'd
shared what had happened with his brother and although he knew Rich wouldn't have blabbed it, the
rest of the family, or even those in town, could easily put it all together. They all knew he'd been gone
at the same time as the attack, and they knew his
background in Special Forces. Two plus two still
equaled four in West Bend.

Rich shook his head. "But you just know she's
here sniffing out a story and who's a bigger story
right now than you? You should leave before it's too
late and don't come back into town until she's gone."

"Great, I'll be exiled from my own hometown."

Rich touched his shoulder, pulling Quinn's attention to him. "It's better than having your face
splashed all over every television in America."

Quinn thought again about Rizzo and the press
he was generating these days. His brother was right.
He needed to stay as far away from Dana Lang as
he could.

Dana walked to the library, where her journey
here had started. She'd made friends with the head
librarian, Lila, a wiry, bespectacled woman in her
fifties and the first friendly face she'd encountered
in town and, if yesterday's events were any indication, the only friendly face she would see besides
Quinn Dawson. But she wouldn't be dissuaded. She'd

faced opposition before on cases she'd investigated and she'd persevered. This would be no different.

Lila's face lit up when Dana entered the library. She hurried around the main desk and pulled Dana into a hug. "I heard what happened to you last night," she said. "Did you get hurt?"

She was a little shocked that the news had spread so fast, but then remembered small towns were notorious for everyone knowing everyone else's business. "I'm fine. He didn't take anything. Just spray-painted a nasty note on my hotel wall."

"I feel responsible since I'm the one who recommended that hotel. It's normally a perfectly safe place."

She glanced at Lila and realized she was the only person besides the hotel clerk and the sheriff's office who knew Dana was in town investigating this case. "Did you tell anyone where I was staying or what I was looking in to?"

Lila's face reddened and she began stammering. "I might have mentioned it to a few folks when I was getting coffee yesterday afternoon. I'm sorry, Dana. I was excited to have a big-time television star in our town. I guess I was bragging. It felt good to have people think I was helping you."

Dana sighed as she realized Lila probably hadn't meant for anything bad to happen to her. But someone had heard what she was up to and decided to take matters into their own hands.

"Do you remember who was at the coffee shop yesterday?"

"Not really. Why?"

"Well, someone heard you. If I can figure out who, I might be able to track down the person who broke into my room."

Lila's face flushed. "Oh, well, then I suppose you'd also have to have the names of everyone at the grocery store and the beauty shop and everyone who came into the library yesterday. I might have mentioned it more than I let on."

Dana smiled past her annoyance and tried to reassure her. "That's okay. So basically, anyone could have heard about it." You had to love the small-town grapevine. She tried another tactic. "Did anyone seem overly concerned about me being in town? Maybe someone asked a lot of questions about what I was working on?"

"Everyone was curious, of course, but I can't think of anyone who would want to do you harm."

She could see this was a dead end. It didn't matter who had heard the news—she imagined by this point everyone in town knew it.

"Did you locate the microfiche I asked for?"

"I did. I'll show you where they're at." Lila crossed the main floor and Dana followed her. Microfiche wasn't used much anymore but Dana was surprised when Lila led her through the side door and up a flight of stairs. She'd expected it to be in an out-of-the-way place, like the basement.

She shot Lila a questioning glance.

"We had it downstairs until a pipe burst last year and flooded the basement. We moved the machine upstairs to a storage closet behind the stacks. It's a little dark but it's private. No one should bother you."

She followed Lila through rows of shelves lined with books until they reached a door on the far wall. Lila unlocked the door and Dana stepped inside. The room was filled with boxes and supplies. In the corner was the microfiche machine with a chair pushed up to it. A fluorescent light flickered overhead, threatening to go out at any moment. Lila was right about it being private. Few people would venture here except by accident. But she'd faced worse circumstances and she wasn't going to complain. "I'll be fine. Thank you, Lila."

She motioned to a box of microfiche next to the machine. "I pulled everything I could find on the murders for you. And the machine is set up to print to the circulation-desk printer downstairs. I'll be around if you need anything."

Lila disappeared into the stacks while Dana set down her purse and got to work. She pulled out the first microfiche film and placed it into the machine. She scrolled through the newspaper dates until she came to the front-page headline on the day after the murders: Double Murder Stuns West Bend.

The article went on to describe how the local volunteer fire department had responded to the fire at the Renfield home. One body had been discovered, that of Mrs. Rene Renfield. Police were being tight-lipped about how she died, but it was rumored that she was already deceased when the fire was started. The whereabouts of Paul Renfield and the couple's one-year-old daughter, Alicia, had yet to be determined.

Dana knew from the article in her mom's belongings, dated six days later, that the child's body would not be found for two more days, when it was discovered beneath rubble of the house by fireman Jay Englin, but she doubted the veracity of that report, believing the local authorities, namely Sheriff Mackey, had covered up the fact that Alicia—that *Dana*—was alive. Was she found in the rubble of the house two days after the fire as this article stated? It seemed unlikely. She would have been severely dehydrated and suffering smoke inhalation at the least, and been taken immediately to the hospital, where several people would have seen her, making a cover-up unlikely. How then, and more importantly *when,* did Jay Englin find her?

She wished she could track him down, but so far, she hadn't been able to find a current address or online presence for him. He was the one person still living who could confirm that a child's body had actually been discovered. She thought about asking Lila if she had any information on Jay's whereabouts. She wasn't giving up on talking to him and would continue trying to locate him.

She printed out several articles that mentioned the murders and jotted down every piece of information she could find about the details of the case, hoping the reporters who'd written for the paper back then had better access to the police files than she did. Perhaps she could even track down one of them for an interview. She glanced at the bylines and realized most of the articles were written by two people, Jerry Foster and Jane Shaw. She added their names to her list of people she wanted to interview. It would be nice to speak to them to discover if there was anything in their notes that hadn't made it into the articles.

She took out her phone and looked up the paper on-line, only to discover it had folded back in the late nineties, when the digital age began to make papers around the country flounder. It was no surprise that a small-town paper couldn't make it. There was, however, a webpage that seemed active. She clicked the link and discovered Jerry Foster still operated an online blog. She skimmed through the archives and found no mention of the murder, but if he was still writing then perhaps he would remember the case. She quickly pulled up her email and shot him a message asking to meet.

Suddenly, the room went dark. The machine shut down, and only the light from her phone illuminated the room. The machine was old and probably hadn't been used in a while. Perhaps it had blown a fuse. She opened the door and found the lights were off in the stacks as well, and it was dark as night as she made her way toward the light she saw filtering in through the windows in the main area.

She cleared the stacks and looked around. No one was here, but the hairs on the back of her neck suddenly raised and Dana swore she felt eyes on her, watching her. She glanced around and saw no one, yet she couldn't shake the eerie feeling that she wasn't alone. She pressed the button for the elevator, then realized it wasn't working, either.

Rubbing her arms, that feeling of being watched was strong. Someone was up here with her, but why weren't they showing themselves? "Hello?" she called, watching for movement and feeling silly for the uneasiness washing over her. It was probably Lila or one of the other librarians reshelving or straightening books. Sure they were. In the dark. "Hello?" she called again.

No one responded.

A door slammed and she jumped and spun around. Someone had just left through the side door that led downstairs. But why hadn't they answered when she'd called?

She hurried over and pushed open the door, "Who's there?" she called, her voice echoing through the stairwell. "I know someone was just here. Who is it?"

She started down the steps. The lights were out here, too, but if someone was trying to frighten her they'd have to do a better job than spying on her at the library or cutting power to the microfiche. She wasn't going to be intimidated.

In the darkness, she felt a hand on her back, shoving her. She went tumbling down the concrete steps, pain shooting through her with every bump. She hit the bottom, jamming her shoulder into the concrete floor. Her head spun, but she forced herself to glance up, pain shooting through her as she did. All she saw was darkness above her. A figure moved at the top of the stairs but she couldn't make it out. Man or woman? Young or old? She couldn't tell. Then the darkness pulled her away and she didn't know anything else.

TWO

Quinn was still thinking about Dana Lang by the time he returned home. He'd been to the post office, the barber shop and the grocery store since leaving the sheriff's office and it seemed the beautiful television reporter was all anyone in town wanted to talk about. No wonder he couldn't push her from his mind.

The woman had spunk, that was for certain, and he liked that. Although he was glad to learn that she wasn't in town sniffing around the embassy story or his connection to it, he didn't like having her here at all. She was looking for shock and awe in order to make a name for herself. Well, she wasn't going to use his family to do it.

He picked up a photograph of him and his grandfather taken by the lake when he was twelve. He'd loved that man with all his heart and the feeling had been mutual. They'd spent every moment together— when they weren't at school or work—and during summers Quinn had practically lived at his grandparents' house, at least until his mother forced him to return home for a few days. Then he was right back.

That man had taught him everything he knew about mechanics and fishing and hunting, but he'd also taught him important things like integrity and honor and faith. It burned him up that someone like Dana Lang would try to mar a good man's name all for the sake of a story.

Quinn remembered the Renfield case. His grandfather had spoken often about how brutal the attack on the wife had been. It was only one of a few cases during his career that had haunted him, especially the death of the little girl. His grandfather had once told Quinn he thought about her regularly and wished he could have done more to help her.

Quinn probably still had his grandfather's personal files, brought from the sheriff's office after his death, but Dana wasn't going to get her hands on them. He knew there was a file on that case because his grandfather had looked at it every so often and tried to see if he could figure out what happened to the father, or if there were any clues he missed about the man's whereabouts.

Quinn shook his head. Dana had planted doubts in his head and he had to address them. He took out the bible his grandfather had given him on his eighteenth birthday and opened it to the inscription on the front page.

Quinn, let these words be your guide. Love, Grandpa.

He stared at the handwriting and felt his heart drop. He hadn't been imagining it. His grandfather's rich script was easily distinguishable. If it wasn't his writing on that note, then someone had done a good imitation.

What did you do, Grandpa?

Had he really abandoned a child, and if he had, why? And more importantly, had that child been Alicia Renfield? He wished for the millionth time that his grandfather was here with him so he could ask. Quinn missed his wisdom and guidance, especially since his life had gotten so topsy-turvy with the embassy attack, losing Tommy and Mike and now Dana Lang arriving in town.

He opened the bible to his grandfather's favorite passage, Hebrews 11:1 and read the words aloud. "'Now faith is the substance of things hoped for, the evidence of things not seen.'"

Quinn wanted to take comfort in this verse, the way his is grandfather always had. He'd believed in his own faith, but the last several months had left him wondering. The evidence he was seeing was sending his life spiraling out of control, and now Dana had added another layer to it with her investigation into his grandfather. He rubbed his face. His grandfather had professed to be a man of faith and Quinn had never seen evidence to doubt that. He wouldn't start doubting now, not unless he had a lot more proof of wrongdoing.

His phone rang and he scooped it up, checking the ID. It was his brother. "Hey, Rich, what's up?"

"I thought you might like to know we just responded to an incident at the library involving your Dana Lang."

"Was she hurt?" He grimaced at the question. Why should he care? She was out to destroy his family.

"Not seriously. She claims someone pushed her down the stairs. She has some bumps and bruises, but she's mostly all right. Here's the thing, though. Someone intentionally cut the power to the top floor. Sliced the wires right in two. The librarian didn't see anyone coming or going and she can account for everyone that was there. First the graffiti in Lang's hotel room and now this. Do you think she might be orchestrating all this in order to build up the story she's working on?"

"No, that doesn't seem like her style." He hated to defend her, but he'd been with her at the hotel. He'd seen the way her hands shook and the fear in her expression. She hadn't been faking that. "I know the library doesn't have security cameras, but the ATM at the bank across the street might have a clear view of whoever was coming and going from there. Can you see if you can pull their security feed?"

Rich sighed. "I'm already on it. Talk to you later."

Quinn ended the call, but he kept replaying their conversation in his head. He didn't believe Dana was making all this up for a story. He'd seen enough fear during his years with Delta that he could recognize true terror when he saw it. Someone was after her, but what was there about the Renfield case that someone would want to hide? It had gone cold a very long time ago.

Still, it couldn't be a coincidence that she'd come to town to investigate this murder and now someone was targeting her. She didn't strike him as the type of woman to turn and run, either. She was going to dig in to this case, and while he knew his grandfather hadn't been involved in any criminal act, Dana Lang was an unknown factor. He grabbed his keys. It wouldn't hurt to check up on her. For his own peace of mind, he wanted to know that his grandfather would not be her fall guy.

Dana grimaced as the doctor poked and prodded her arm then tried to move it into different positions. It hurt, but she didn't believe anything was permanently damaged, and after the examination, the doctor concurred.

"Your X-rays are fine and you have good range of motion. It looks like you jarred that shoulder when you fell. I'll write you a prescription for some pain medicine and you'll probably want to ice it, but I think it'll feel better in a few days. However, I do have some concerns over your head injury. You have a mild concussion. I'd recommend you take it easy for at least twenty-four hours. No handling heavy machinery, and that includes driving."

She reluctantly agreed and thanked the doctor, who then left the exam room. Her head did sort of feel like it was spinning. Besides, she didn't even have her rental car with her. It was still parked in the lot at the library. Surely, she could find a cab to take her back to her hotel, order in room service and spend yet another night wondering who was targeting her and why.

Someone had been there, trying to intimidate her, and she remembered the feel of his hand on her back, pushing her forward. And he'd cut the power to the floor she was working on. Two attacks in two days? This wasn't random.

A nurse came in to help her get dressed. Dana was glad to be released after hours of being examined.

"I'll go start your release paperwork," the nurse said, then left her alone to gather her things.

She picked up her phone. The screen had cracked in the fall, but thankfully it was still operational. She had a message from Tracy, her friend and research assistant, who wanted to know how her investigation was proceeding, and another from her producer wanting some additional information about stories that they were preparing to air.

One message stood out, however. It was a reply from Jerry Foster, the reporter she'd emailed and asked for an interview. He'd agreed to her request and asked for her to meet him at his home in Bedford, twenty miles away, at 8:00 p.m. tonight. She glanced at the time on her phone and realized it was already after seven. She would never make it in time unless she could find a cab that would drive her that far. She typed up a quick response, letting him know she was coming but that she might be a little late. She'd just hit Send on the email when someone grabbed her from behind. A hand clamped over her mouth and the blade of a knife dug into her neck. Startled, she dropped the phone and grabbed for her assailant's hand, trying to pull it away.

"You're sticking your nose where it doesn't belong," a voice hissed in her ear. "If you know what's good for you, you'll pack up and leave town today."

"Here we go," the nurse said, walking back into the room with papers in hand. She screamed when she saw the man with the knife.

Suddenly, he shoved Dana, sending her reeling into a chair and taking down a bedside lamp as she fell. She hit the floor, landing hard on her knee and jarring that shoulder once again. When she looked up, a hooded figure was barreling past the nurse and exiting the room.

Dana tried to etch an image of him into her memory so she could describe her attacker to the police, but her head was spinning too much.

Then another figure appeared in the doorway, hesitating for a moment before rushing to her side.

Quinn.

"Dana, what happened? Are you okay?"

"He grabbed me, Quinn. He snuck up behind me and grabbed me. He put a knife to my throat." She didn't like the high-pitched fearful way her voice sounded, but she couldn't control her emotions right now. Shock and fear were too strong for her to deny. If the nurse hadn't returned with her papers, what would he have done to her?

"Who did that?" he demanded. "The guy in the hoodie?"

She must have managed to nod or somehow signal *yes* because he took off, stopping only to check that the nurse was okay before he ran from the room and disappeared into the hall.

Dana pulled herself into a chair. She couldn't stop the sobs that rushed through her at the memory of those terrifying seconds of not knowing what was going to happen. She put her face into her hands and let the tears come.

Quinn spotted the hooded figure ducking into the stairwell and he followed. Seeing Dana on the floor pushed him forward. The assailant could have killed her right then and Quinn would have been seconds too late to do anything to help her.

Too late, just as he'd been for Tommy.

Anger lit through him. This guy had to be stopped.

Quinn pushed through the door and saw the man below him on the stairs.

"Hey!" Quinn shouted.

The guy looked up at him, then took off down the stairs.

Quinn chased after him. Whoever this guy was, he was fast and agile. He got to the bottom and burst through the door to the lobby, but by the time Quinn reached it, the man was pushing his way out the front doors and shoving aside anyone who dared to step into his path. Quinn tried to follow him but the guy was too fast. Frustration rattled him as he realized he might lose the guy. What he wouldn't give for his sniper's rifle right about now. He'd end this guy's getaway with a single shot.

He pushed through the front doors of the hospital as the attacker sprinted across the parking lot and ducked into the woods. Quinn stopped running, realizing he wasn't going to catch him. The guy was too fast.

He leaned over, resting his hands on his knees, and tried to catch his breath. He usually trained every day, even when he was home, but since the embassy attack and Tommy's death, he hadn't had the desire to work out and it showed today. This short sprint had taken a lot of out of him.

He returned to the third floor, glad to see that security had been called and was busy securing the floor. He stopped one of the guards and told him who he was and about the hooded figure he'd tried to apprehend.

"Check the security tapes. Maybe one of them got an image of his face."

While the guy had glanced up when Quinn shouted, the hood had masked his face and Quinn couldn't give a better description than height and weight and color of the hoodie he was wearing.

The guard nodded and relayed the information to his supervisor over the radio.

Quinn walked into Dana's room and saw her on the bed being examined by the nurses. Her eyes held a sunken look to them as if she'd been defeated. He supposed she had been, but it could have been much worse. He could have walked into this room to find her dead with her throat slashed.

She perked up when she spotted him. "Quinn! Did you catch him?"

He hated to wipe away the look of hope on her face. "No, he got away." He mentally kicked himself. He should have continued training, not spent time mourning what he'd lost. What good had that done him? He was supposed to be a hero. Isn't that what all the news channels were calling them for disobeying orders and charging into the embassy to rescue those trapped inside? But he didn't feel like much of a hero today. "What happened?" he asked her.

"I don't know. I was turned away looking at my phone and the next thing I knew, he'd grabbed me. I didn't even hear him come in. He told me I was sticking my nose where it didn't belong and that I should pack up and leave town."

Another threat to give up her investigation and leave? He'd obviously been wrong in assuming no one would care she was looking into a thirty-year-old cold case. Someone apparently cared a lot. But who and why?

Whatever it was, he was going to find out.

"How is she?" he asked, directing this question to the nurse.

"She landed hard on that shoulder again, but other than that, she's going to be fine."

"Good." He turned back to Dana. "I'm going downstairs to check out the security video, but I'll be back soon."

He left her in the care of the nurse and walked downstairs, taking a moment to phone his brother to let the sheriff's office know what had happened.

"Was she hurt?" Rich asked after Quinn had explained.

"Not seriously, but she could have been."

"Okay, you check out the security feeds to see if you can ID this guy and I'll let Dad know. I'll also watch for any suspicious sightings of a guy in a hoodie matching that height and weight. Keep me posted."

"I will," Quinn assured him.

He spoke with the head of security, showed his credentials as a reserve deputy and asked for an update. They had little to offer.

One of the security techs pulled up the video. "We were able to capture images of this guy as he moved throughout the hospital, but none of them show his face. Even before he attacked her, he was keeping his face hidden from the cameras."

"He knew what he was doing," Quinn stated. "Were you able to backtrack to look at what kind of vehicle he arrived in?"

The tech shook his head. "No, the first image we have of him is in the parking lot."

Quinn hated how careful this guy was being. "Keep watching the parking lot. If he had a car, he'll eventually have to come back for it."

The security tech assured Quinn he would keep watching, and Quinn walked back upstairs to check on Dana. He hated that he didn't have better news to give her. Whoever had attacked her had once again managed to get away clean.

He was surprised to find her dressed in her street clothes and the nurse helping her with her shoes, as if she was getting ready to leave the hospital. "What are you doing?"

"I'm leaving. I have a meeting with Jerry Foster tonight."

"Who is Jerry Foster?"

"A former writer at the *West Bend Daily News*. In fact, I'd confirmed I was on my way when that guy grabbed me. If I hurry, I can still make it."

"You can't leave. I'm sure they need to keep you overnight." He looked to the nurse for confirmation but she shook her head.

"Actually, she's free to go. I was working on her discharge papers before this happened and although her knee is bruised up, I don't see anything that would necessitate keeping her overnight." She touched Dana's shoulder. "I do recommend you take it easy, though. You've been through something terrible with these two attacks."

"I will. I promise I'll take it easy, but I must do this interview. Can you arrange a cab for me?"

"Sure, I'll call one for you," the nurse agreed.

Quinn couldn't believe what he was hearing. They were letting her go? Didn't they realize how dangerous that could be? He knew it wasn't the hospital's job to protect her, but he would feel better knowing she was safe and sound in a hospital room overnight with a deputy posted on her door.

But that obviously wasn't happening, which didn't leave him with much of a choice. "That won't be necessary," he said. "I'll drive you."

He wasn't letting her go off on her own again, not until they found out who was threatening her and why.

Dana hurried through the paperwork the nurse gave her then reluctantly allowed herself to be wheeled to the front doors of the hospital in a wheelchair.

"I don't need this," she insisted. "I can walk myself." However, the nurse claimed it was hospital policy and refused to bend the rules.

Dana was a little surprised to see Quinn waiting for her, his truck parked by the front doors and the passenger door open. But she was more surprised by his insistence on driving her to her interview with Mr. Foster. Was he so worried about her safety that he didn't want to let her out of his sight? She didn't know whether to be terrified or flattered by that prospect.

She pushed herself up from the wheelchair only to fall back into it as dizziness overtook her. She hated the feeling of weakness that flowed through her and hated even more that Quinn was seeing her at her most vulnerable. She was trying hard to maintain a semblance of strength and determination, but she had to admit she was exhausted.

"Let me help you," he said, his strong arms suddenly around her as she stood again. She glanced up into his soft green eyes and saw compassion there. He really was a good man and she was thankful he was here for her.

She leaned on him for support, her head woozy at the sudden loss of balance, or maybe the feel of his embrace. She was close enough to smell the musky scent of his aftershave and feel the muscles in his arms as they tightened around her. It had been too long since she'd been in a man's arms. Not since her relationship with Jason Webber had ended six months ago. But then she'd never felt as protected in his embrace as she did right now in Quinn's.

"You okay?" he asked, helping her steady herself.

She gave a brief nod. "I'm fine." But the way her head spun had nothing to do with her mild concussion.

His arms loosened around her, but he didn't move away. "You sure?" She sensed his patience and protectiveness. He wouldn't let go until she was steady.

What was she doing getting all moony over Quinn Dawson? She was acting like a child with a crush on a man who'd swooped in and saved her life. She had to get a grip before she made a complete fool of herself. He might seem like a good guy, and maybe he was, but she'd learned the hard way that love and family weren't in her future. She'd been left and abandoned too many times to allow her heart to be broken again. Even God had left her years ago and if He didn't want her, why would someone like Quinn Dawson? She wouldn't—couldn't—go down that road again. "I'm okay," she assured him, then stepped up into his truck, his hand never leaving her until she was safely seated inside.

He crawled in behind the wheel then started the truck, but tried one more time to change her mind. "Isn't this something that can wait until tomorrow? I know you're hot on this story, but it's a thirty-year-old case. It will keep one more day."

She shook her head then grimaced at the pain that caused. "One thing I've learned in this business is that if someone agrees to be interviewed, it's better not to give them the time to change their minds. Besides, someone's trying to frighten me into giving up. I don't want to give them time to get to Jerry Foster, too." She wondered if Quinn was already regretting offering to drive her. If he'd been expecting an argument, he was disappointed. She was desperate and she was holding him to his proposition to drive her.

He gave her a look that said he couldn't believe she was being so reckless, but he put the truck into gear and took off down the road without saying a word.

The last time they'd been alone together, she'd opened her mouth and accused his grandfather of something awful. She had to admit she was curious to know after that incident why he was helping her.

"I'm sorry if I upset you last night. I didn't mean to imply anything about your grandfather. I'm really just searching for the truth."

He nodded. "My grandfather was a good man, Dana. You didn't know him, but he was. He loved his family, this town and he loved the Lord. He always taught me to be a man of honor."

She saw the love he had for his grandfather and admired it, but she also knew that people often did things that surprised those who loved them. She saw it all the time in her investigations for *Newswatch*. How many wives and families had ever suspected their fathers or brothers or uncles of being cold-blooded serial killers? They were always the ones surprised by the revelations when the truth came out. She'd lived it, too, in her relationship with Jason, who'd fooled her into thinking he loved her then betrayed her.

"I know you want to believe that, but in my experience, that's hardly ever the case."

"I just want to make sure that you don't have tunnel vision in this matter. It seems like you've focused in on him. My family isn't the story."

She remained silent on the rest of the drive. She was sorry that Quinn thought she was targeting his family, but finding out the truth about her identity and what really happened to Alicia Renfield was all that mattered to her now, not Quinn Dawson's feelings, or anyone else's. She was on a mission to find answers and it was one she was determined to see through.

"Thank you for meeting with me," Dana said when Jerry Foster invited them both inside.

"Glad to do it," he said.

"This is Quinn Dawson. He's going to sit in, if you don't mind."

"Not at all." He reached out to shake Quinn's hand. "I'm familiar with your family. I don't know your father well, but I knew your grandfather. He was a good man."

"Yes, he was," Quinn responded, shaking the man's hand and giving Dana a sideways, told-you-so glance. "Thank you for saying it."

Jerry shut the front door, then motioned for them to follow him into the kitchen, where he went to the coffeepot and filled three cups. "Have a seat," he said, handing them each a mug.

Dana took it from his hand and sat down, anxious to ask her questions before her fuzzy, concussed brain let them get away, but she'd learned from experience that it was always better to get people talking about themselves before digging into serious questions. "Tell me about the newspaper. How long did you work there?"

"I did more than work there, miss. I owned it. It was a family business, started by my father in 1935. He passed it on to me. We had our good years and our bad ones, but it became too much when everything started going digital. I kept an online paper going for a while, but I finally gave that up a few years ago, too, and retired completely when my wife got ill, except for an occasional blog post now and then."

"I'm sorry about your wife. How is she?"

"She passed away last year. Cancer. Jane and I were together for forty-three years."

Dana's ears perked up at the familiar name. "Jane Shaw? I recognize her name from the byline of the articles I read. She wrote for the paper, too."

Jerry nodded. "Yes, she did. She was already

a writer when we met in college and she kept her maiden name. She was a valuable asset to the paper. I couldn't have kept it going all those years without her. She was smart as well as beautiful."

Dana was sad to hear about her passing. Jane Shaw had been on her list of people to question about the murders. "I'm sorry for your loss," she told Jerry, and she meant it. It was obvious he'd lost his entire world in the past few years. She knew what that felt like.

He tapped his finger on the table and locked eyes with her, his face morphing from a grieving widower to the newspaperman he'd once been. "But you didn't come here to talk about me and my family, did you, Miss Lang? You want to know about the murders."

Excitement bubbled through her. This was why she'd come to town and finally she was going to have answers to her questions. She tried to keep her excitement hidden as she nodded. "Do you remember it?"

"Every detail. My body isn't as sharp as it used to be, but I still have my mind."

"What can you tell me about it?"

"I remember the night of the fire," he told her. "It was around eight when I heard on the police scanner about a fire out there at the Renfield place. By the time I arrived, the fire department couldn't do much except keep it contained to the house. They didn't want it to spread to the brush and catch the woods on fire. It was blazing hot and smoke had filled the place. Several of the firemen had tried to go inside to look for survivors but the smoke was too thick and black. They weren't able to see anything."

"Diesel fuel," Quinn stated, and Jerry nodded.

"The family had their own gas tanks. It was once a working plantation and they still had some fields they plowed so they kept fuel on hand."

Dana glanced at Quinn. He was pinching the bridge of his nose and looked to be pained by the tale. How had he known that about the diesel fuel?

"Of course, that was also a sure sign that someone had intentionally set the fire. Regular house fires don't burn like that and the use of an accelerant indicated arson. No one had any idea where the family was, but I remember the garage door was up and both cars were inside. I figured they had to be home. It wasn't until early the next morning that the fire died out enough for anyone to start searching. Rene's body was found inside the house at the foot of the stairs. Some people speculated that she'd been trying to escape the fire…that is, until the coroner discovered she'd been shot."

"I've read all of your and Jane's articles about the fire and murders. How much of what you wrote came from primary sources?"

"We'd never had anything like this happen in West Bend before. No one knew exactly how to handle it. We spoke with the sheriff's office often and they answered our questions. There was an understanding among everyone that the public deserved to know the details."

"What about Bill Mackey? Did he speak directly with you about the case?"

He turned his gaze to Quinn, then tapped his finger. "No, he was pretty tight-lipped about it. Most of our information came from the other deputies. Today it's common for police to keep their stories close to the vest, but it wasn't that way back then, not in West Bend. This was the first case that Sheriff Mackey became very secretive about."

"Did he ever give you a reason for the change?" Quinn asked.

"No, just said the victims deserved some privacy and the investigation was ongoing. There were rumors around town that Rene was planning on leaving Paul and running off with another man, so when his body wasn't recovered, everyone figured he'd killed her then started the fire. His parents had died in an accident a few months earlier and many of Paul's friends refused to believe he could be responsible for killing the only family he had left. They thought he died in the fire and his body hadn't been found yet or else burned up."

"Was there any evidence to back up the story about her leaving Paul?"

"No, only rumors. People said they'd been arguing a lot lately. They didn't know what about, but no one believed things were bad enough for him to kill her over."

"Why do you think the sheriff stopped talking to you?" Dana asked.

The older man shook his head. "I think it had to do with the little girl. Jay Englin found her body a few days later in the rubble. It had to change Bill to see that. That's my opinion. After that, I imagine he changed his mind about what the public needed to know." He shrugged. "He never came out and said that was what it was, but I figured it had to be."

His reasoning seemed logical, but he didn't know Dana suspected Jay Englin had never found the child's body in the rubble. "And what about Jay Englin? How did finding her affect him?"

"It shook him up good. He started drinking after that and eventually quit the fire department. He moved out of state a few years later. Last I heard, he was living in Memphis selling insurance."

She knew that pulling a dead child from a burned home would have to do unspeakable things to someone's emotions. Yet, had that really been the reason for their changes in attitude? If Dana was right, he hadn't really done that, so it shouldn't have affected him that way. But something had shaken him based on Jerry's account of his change in behavior. What had he really seen that night? Something that suggested the baby was in too much danger to let anyone believe she was alive? Dana carefully broached her next question. "Did someone besides Jay Englin and Bill Mackey ever see the child's body?"

He gave her a questioning look. "I don't really know the answer to that. The coroner did, I'm sure, but he died a long time ago."

"Did you ever see the body?"

"No, of course not. Not sure I would have wanted to. Jane and I attended the funerals, however, for both Rene and little Alicia. I'll tell you both, seeing that little bitty coffin about did me in. I can't imagine what Bill and Jay felt."

"What can you tell me about the circumstances of Jay Englin finding the child's body? Was he searching with a group of people? Did he call anyone over to see what he'd found?"

"As far as I can remember, he was out there by himself. Everyone else had already given up on searching through the rubble, but he wouldn't. He was determined to find her. Of course, by that time, the coroner had done the autopsy and discovered Rene had been killed by a gunshot. There were already more rumors swirling around that Paul had shot Rene and taken off with the child. You probably know they never did find Paul, so that was a logical assumption. But then Jay found the little girl. He called Bill and that was that."

No one else had actually seen the child. That only reinforced Dana's belief. But if everyone already assumed Paul had taken off with Alicia, why the elaborate charade of Jay finding her body in the rubble and faking her death? Why not stick to the story and allow Alicia Renfield to be merely a child kidnapped by her murderer father?

Of course, it was also possible that her father was the very one to abandon her at that church in his hurry to get away. Perhaps he'd killed Rene in a fit of rage then come to his senses and decided he couldn't take his baby daughter on the run with him.

But that didn't explain the note written in Bill Mackey's handwriting or the preacher's letter saying someone he trusted had dropped off the baby and said she was in danger.

She needed to find Jay Englin. He was the only one still alive who could provide answers.

She asked Jerry Foster a few more questions, then brought up the one subject that gave her pause. "Was there any real evidence that connected Paul to the murders?" If her suspicions were true and she was Alicia Renfield, that meant her own father might have killed her mother. It was a lot to wrap her head around and she didn't want to jump to the conclusion without reason, despite what everyone else believed. Her work was based on facts, not long-held conjecture.

"All I know is there was evidence of murder and Paul was nowhere to be found. If the police discovered actual evidence that implicated him, they didn't share it."

And without access to the police records, she might never find it. Back to square one. She chatted with him for a few minutes about the paper and how the town had changed in the past thirty years before thanking him for his help.

"I understand your fascination with this case," Jerry told her. "But I doubt you're going to uncover anything groundbreaking. If you can find Paul Renfield and make him pay for what he did that night, that would be good. I, for one, would like to know why he did it. Motive is the one question that's haunted me all these years about that case. I can believe jealousy might lead a man to kill his wife, but why the baby?"

"I hope I can answer that question for you, Jerry, and maybe even a few others you didn't even know to ask." Someone wanted her to stop investigating, which meant someone in this town was hiding something to do with this case. There were answers out there to be found, and she was intent on finding them.

She thanked him for speaking with her and he shook both their hands before they left.

Once they were out the door, Quinn turned to her, his tone sharp. "What was that?"

"What was what?"

"Why were you asking so many questions about how they found Alicia Renfield? I thought you didn't believe she died. Didn't you say someone left her at a church a few days later?"

She followed him to the truck, where he opened the passenger-side door. "There's no way she was lying in the rubble all that time until Jay Englin found her. Something else happened that night and I want to know what it is. The only way I can do that is to blow holes in the official story." But if Jerry Foster couldn't give her the real story, how would she ever find it? She got inside but turned to him before he shut the door, hoping he could help here more than he realized. "I really wish I could have a look at the investigative records or even your grandfather's notes on the case. He must have had a reason for covering all this up."

He narrowed his eyes at her as if trying to read her. "My grandfather was a good man, Dana." He slammed the truck door, then walked around and slid into the driver's seat. She'd hit a nerve.

"Tell me about him. Help me get to know him. He

was a major player in this case. There's no denying that. The more I know about him, the better I can form my opinions."

"He's not your story," he replied curtly, then turned back in his seat and started the truck. He was obviously not ready to talk about his grandfather to her.

As they drove, she broached another subject she wanted to ask him about. "How did you know about the diesel fuel used to start the fire?"

His jaw clenched and his hands gripped the steering wheel. He was suddenly on guard again at such a simple question. "I've seen something like it," he said, but he didn't elaborate. He was obviously holding something back, which only made the reporter in her itch to know more.

"In the military?"

He paled. "What?" He shot her a look of confusion that she didn't believe. He was definitely holding something back, something he didn't want her to know. It disappointed her to see the change in him, but it didn't surprise her. He was already guarded with her about his grandfather. Perhaps he now believed she might turn her focus to him if he told her too much about his past. She tried not to take it personally. Most of the people she interviewed were watchful about what they said because they never knew if their deepest darkest secrets would be televised. But she wasn't in town as a reporter and she wasn't working a case for her show. He might not know that, but his mistrust stung.

"I've been around military men before, Quinn. What branch were you in?"

He gripped the steering wheel again but this time gave her an answer. "I was in the army. Look, Dana, I don't really like to talk about myself. If you don't mind, I'd prefer it if you dropped the subject."

He must have seen combat, she realized. She'd interviewed many soldiers whose experiences in combat had caused them to shut down. In fact, he reminded her so much of the way Rizzo had been during their first meeting, closed off and distant. It wasn't any surprise to find that Quinn didn't want to discuss his time in the military with her. She nodded and accepted his request without hesitation. "Of course," she said, but it saddened her because she did want to get to know this man. He had a protective nature that she found appealing and she admired the way he stood up for his family. And she appreciated his willingness to help her. She only wanted to know him better and she realized it had nothing at all to do with the case she was working on.

It was probably for the best, though. She wasn't looking for a relationship. They always ended with her getting hurt. "Mind if I turn on the radio?" she asked, needing to fill the awkward silence in the cab.

He nodded that it was fine and she reached over and hit the knob. The radio was tuned to a news station covering the embassy attack. Finally, something they could discuss that didn't have any implications between them. "Have you heard about this? I was fortunate enough to interview some of the people that were rescued from inside the embassy by security operatives from a nearby covert base. I also interviewed Rizzo Ricardo about his experiences as one of those operatives. They really were heroes. Did you know the government ordered them to not intervene? They wanted to protect their covert operations in the country. Everyone inside that embassy would have died if those eight men hadn't defied orders." Remembering Rizzo's story of that night, she shuddered. Those men had been true heroes, running into the blackest diesel-fuel fires started by insurgents when others would have fled to safety. "I only wish the other operatives would come forward and tell their stories as well. What I wouldn't give to know the names of the other men involved."

His face reddened and his eyes suddenly blazed as he looked at her. "Don't you realize that by coming forward, they would be putting their lives in danger. At the very least, their livelihoods? Once their faces are splashed all over TVs across the world, they would never be able to work covert security again."

She sighed, seeing they were once again on opposite sides of a situation. Big surprise. She should have expected it. It seemed that if she said the world was round, he would argue with her that it was flat. "Something very important happened that night, Quinn. Someone has to be held responsible and these men can shed a light on that tragedy. Don't you want to know who to blame?"

"The ones to blame are the terrorists who attacked

the embassy. Everything else is just politics. Those men did their jobs. I say leave them alone."

"People died, Quinn, and according to Rizzo, the government did nothing to assist. Don't you think the White House has to answer to that?"

He shook his head, a disgusted expression on his face. "You're always looking for the story, aren't you, Dana?"

His accusation stung, but she felt an angry heat rise up her neck. "I only want the truth."

"What makes you think you're entitled to the truth?" He pulled into the hotel parking lot and stopped the truck, kicking it into Park. He turned to her. "This may go against your reporter sensibilities, but the public doesn't have the right to know about everything that happens. Some things are better left alone."

"Not this," she insisted.

"Why not? What gives you the right to dig in to this story?"

"My government did something unthinkable by leaving those people, our people, to die inside that embassy. It's my duty as a citizen to make sure they pay for their lack of action."

"And the Renfield case? What gives you the right to pry into it? This isn't your town. You have no duty here."

She shook her head, amazed that he hadn't yet figured out why she was really in town. "You saw the note written in your grandfather's hand. Where do you think I got that? I found it in my adopted mother's belongings when she died, along with newspaper clippings about the Renfield murders. Don't you get it, Quinn? I was the child that was left at that church thirty years ago. I'm Alicia Renfield."

He sat back in his seat, a look of shock and horror written across his face. She'd thought he'd figured it out by now, but apparently she'd been wrong.

"I want to know the truth. If I'm really her or not, and if I am, I want to know what happened to my parents that night and how I ended up at some church miles away from here."

He leaned into the steering wheel, obviously still trying to wrap his brain around this new piece of information. Would it make a difference to him? She liked having him on her side and hoped this wouldn't change things between them.

He shut off the ignition then opened the door. "Come on. I'll walk you to your room."

No word about helping her or even taking her hand to make sure she was steady this time. She really had shaken him.

They rode the elevator to her new room on the fourth floor in silence but she felt his presence. After all she'd been through today, she was glad to have him by her side and hoped that wouldn't change. She couldn't imagine going back out into the world of West Bend without Quinn Dawson.

It was silly. She'd never needed anyone with her before. But then she realized that wasn't true. She always had someone with her—her producer or a cameraman. She'd gotten so used to it that she hadn't even realized how alone she was on this project until she'd needed someone and Quinn had shown up.

The elevator doors slid open and he walked with her to her room. He spotted something and she felt him tense. He stepped in front of her and stopped her in her tracks, motioning for her to remain quiet. She saw it then, the way her door was ajar. She definitely hadn't left it that way and she'd even placed the Do Not Disturb sign on it to prevent housekeeping from entering.

Someone had been inside her room. Again.

Quinn nudged the door open and his face paled as he looked inside. She rushed to him and pushed past his arm. The room was empty, but over the bed hung one of her publicity photos from her show. It was attached to the wall with a butcher knife through her face and the words *Go Home* sprawled across the bottom. The papers on her evidence wall had been ripped down and torn into pieces, and were lying on the carpet.

Horror and fear bit at her and she turned away quickly and leaned into Quinn's chest. He wrapped a protective arm around her and pulled her close, then moved her until the threatening photo was out of her sight.

"Don't you worry, Dana," he whispered to her. "No one is going to hurt you again. I'm going to make sure of it."

She took comfort in his reassurance. At least she was no longer alone in this.

THREE

Quinn pulled Dana from the room and back down the hall to the elevators. She was shaking and he couldn't blame her. Seeing that image of her with a knife through her face had shaken him, too.

He led her into the lobby and called Milo over to sit with her while he phoned his brother and explained the situation. He turned to look at her, noticing again how fragile she seemed, but she wasn't. She was strong. He'd seen it firsthand. But even strong people had their limits. Would this be the thing that finally sent her away?

This was his town and it had always been a good place to live. He'd imagined one day raising kids here and not having to worry about the dangers of big-city life. But now, it seemed, evil was lurking, watching and waiting for the opportunity to strike, and it had chosen its target.

Rich arrived with a forensics team and Quinn joined him upstairs while they combed through her hotel room, snapping photos of the scene and bagging the knife to test for prints and DNA. He hoped it would be as simple as a fingerprint match, but he doubted it would. Whoever was doing this had been smart. He'd kept his face hidden from the cameras at both the hotel and the hospital. Surely, he'd also worn gloves when staging this display, but they could hope he'd gotten cocky and missed something they could use to track him.

Quinn's brother pulled him aside. "Any ideas who might have done this?"

He shook his head. "No one comes to mind, but it must have something to do with the Renfield case. All this started happening when Dana arrived in town to investigate it."

"That case is thirty years old."

"The guy who attacked her at the hospital told her she was sticking her nose in where it didn't belong. As far as I know, the Renfield case is all she's looked into."

"Quinn, you're not thinking like a cop. It's more likely this has to do with her than with the Renfield case. She's a celebrity and she's on TV. She probably has a stalker who followed her to town."

That was a possibility he hadn't thought of. "She never mentioned a stalker."

"Maybe she didn't even know she had one. He might not have shown himself until she arrived here in town alone. Or maybe it's someone local who saw their opportunity to get to her."

He rubbed a hand over his face. Rich was probably right. It made more sense than that someone who'd gotten away with murder thirty years ago would have a grudge against Dana or some dark secret she might bring to light. Except the threats seemed connected to the case.

"I'll go talk to her," Rich offered. "You should head home. I'll handle this."

"No, I want to stay and make sure everything is okay before I leave."

Rich paused and stared at him. "What are you even doing here with her, Quinn? Are you getting close to this woman?"

"What? No. I was there when she was attacked at the hospital and I wanted to make sure she made it safely to her room tonight. I walked her up." Even to his own mind, his explanation sounded weak. He shouldn't have been at the hospital in the first place and he certainly shouldn't have volunteered to drive her around afterward. He was supposed to be keeping a low profile away from her. Instead, he'd spent the evening with her.

He followed Rich downstairs to where Dana was still sitting in the lobby, an armed deputy nearby watching for trouble. She was finally starting to get some color back into her face and he was glad to see it.

"Dana, you remember my brother, Rich? You two met at the sheriff's department."

She stood and reached for his hand. "Yes, it's nice to see you again."

"You, too. I'm sorry it's under these circumstances." He motioned for Dana to sit, then slid up a chair for himself. Quinn took a seat between them. "Are you up for answering a few questions?"

She pushed a handful of hair behind her ear and nodded. "Sure, I guess I am."

"Why don't we go back to the beginning when this all started."

"The day after I arrived in town, I was at the coffee shop down the street and I thought I sensed someone watching me. That was before I returned here and found the threat spray-painted on the wall."

"You sensed someone was watching you? Did you see anyone?"

"No, no one that seemed suspicious. People stare at me all the time. I'm on TV. Most of the time I can shrug it off, but this felt different. It felt sinister."

Quinn knew Rich's logical mind would have a difficult time with the notion that someone could sense danger around them, but he'd never been in combat, where a person's instincts were often their best ally, and he'd had very few dangerous encounters during his time with the West Bend sheriff's office.

"Have you ever had this feeling before you came to town?"

"Not that I can recall."

"You're a beautiful lady, plus like you said, you're on TV. Have you ever had a stalker?"

"I know we've had some creepy letters sent to the station, but I've never had anything like these threats before." She seemed to understand what his questions were leading to. "You think someone followed me to town, don't you?"

"That's one possibility. Another is that someone here in town has become obsessed with you because of your celebrity."

"No, this has something to do with the Renfield case. Don't you see that ever since I started digging in to the case, the threats began?"

"Who would threaten you over that?"

"Someone who knew Alicia Renfield didn't die that night thirty years ago."

Quinn was surprised Dana admitted that, but not nearly as shocked as his brother. Rich's eyes widened and he glanced at Quinn, probably thinking this revelation had come out of the blue. He stood to leave. "That's an interesting notion, Miss Lang, but—"

"I'm Alicia Renfield." She stood to face him, jutted out her chin and folded her arms.

He gave her a skeptical look then shook his head, dismissing the idea. "No, you're not. Is this some kind of ploy? Are you trying to get more exposure for your show?"

"This has nothing to do with my show. I was abandoned as a baby at a church sixty miles from here just days after Alicia Renfield supposedly died. Whoever placed me there left a note. I found that note last week while going through my adoptive mother's belongings. There was also a letter from the preacher who arranged my adoption. The note was written in your grandfather's handwriting."

"What?"

"It's true, Rich," Quinn chimed in as he stood up. "I saw it when I responded to the first break-in. I couldn't believe it at first. I even looked at the dedication he wrote in my bible. It was definitely Grandpa's writing."

"Which means your grandfather somehow saved me from that fire, then faked my death and covered it up."

"I don't believe it." Rich looked at Quinn. "You aren't buying in to this story, are you? Grandpa wouldn't have done something like that."

"I think he did," Quinn confessed. "And the fact that someone is now trying to stop Dana from investigating proves he was right to do it."

He could see the wheels in Rich's mind spinning. "Who else knows about this?"

"No one, as far as I know, except the person who broke in and saw the letter. I haven't shown it to anyone except Quinn, who saw the copy pinned to my wall. I have the originals in my briefcase. Come upstairs with me and let me prove it to you."

Rich stared at her for several moments, and Quinn couldn't tell what he was going to do. He knew his brother, and Rich was thinking the most logical choice had to be the correct one until the evidence pointed him in another direction. Finally, he shook his head. "I'll look at your evidence, Miss Lang, but that doesn't mean I'm buying in to this story. If someone is targeting you, it's because of something happening now, not something that happened a lifetime ago." He closed his notebook and slipped it into his pocket. "You can send whatever you want me to see with my brother while I go do some investigating. Don't worry. We'll catch this guy and you'll see it has nothing to do with that case."

He walked away, stopping to chat with a member of the forensics team who'd come downstairs.

She watched him walk away. "He doesn't believe me."

"He's a good cop and he'll do whatever he can to find the person who's trying to harm you, even if he doesn't think it has anything to do with the case."

She turned and stared at him, her brown eyes pleading. "Do you believe me, Quinn?"

He looked at her and couldn't lie. Instead, he took her elbow. "Let me walk you back upstairs and make sure you're locked safely inside."

Disappointment glowed in her eyes, but she didn't press him for an answer. She allowed him to lead her upstairs. He checked her room, then said goodbye at the door before she closed it and he heard the locks click into place.

The truth was, he wasn't sure whether all this had anything to do with the Renfield case. Rich's scenario made sense and had planted doubts in his mind about the attacker's motivations. All he knew for certain was that someone was out to frighten and impede Dana Lang, and he was going to do everything in his power to make sure that didn't happen.

Dana paced back and forth in her hotel room. She'd already showered, doing her best to wash off the icky feeling she'd gotten from this day. She stopped in front of the mirror and stared at the bruises that were forming on her neck where the attacker had grabbed her. She remembered the feel of his hot breath as he whispered his threat into her ear. *You're sticking your nose where it doesn't belong. If you know what's good for you, you'll pack up and leave town today.* She shuddered at that memory, then grabbed her laptop and tried to turn her concentration toward work. She had several emails from her producer she needed to take care of, and it was the perfect excuse to get her mind off her day.

Had she made a mistake in coming here?

That thought raced through her mind even as she tried to push it away. She didn't want to go down that road. Finally, after several false starts on an email, she set aside her laptop. She wasn't going to get any work done tonight. She couldn't concentrate. She was too keyed up. She longed to walk down the street to the coffee shop for a drink and a muffin, but fear of doing so stopped her. Besides, this wasn't the big city. She doubted the coffee shop was even open this time of night. She hated the fear that raced through her at the thought of walking out of this hotel alone. It made her feel weak, like a captive. She needed something—anything—that would make her feel normal again.

The bible on the nightstand called to her. She wished she could pick it up and find comfort in its words the way she'd heard so many people claim they did. She'd interviewed countless people whose faith had seen them through great losses. But God had never been on Dana's side. He'd allowed terrible things to alter her life. Her father's death. Her mother's distance. Even Jason's empty promises that had left her shattered. And now learning she'd been given away as an infant. What kind of God would leave her so alone in life?

She grabbed her phone. She wanted to talk to someone and knew Tracy would still be up. She was a night owl that rarely slept. She quickly dialed the number and was relieved when her friend answered.

"How's it going, Dana?" Tracy asked in her usual sunny voice.

Dana suddenly realized she couldn't tell Tracy what had been happening. Her friend would insist that Dana return home immediately and she wasn't going to do that. "I'm restless," she said instead. "Can't sleep. Tell me what's been going on with you?"

Her friend told her about several funny incidents that had happened to her the last few days and listening to her chatter energized Dana and gave her a renewed confidence about what she was doing. She'd come here for answers and she was going to get them no matter what.

She wouldn't allow someone with a grudge against her, or something to hide, stop her from finding out the truth about her identity.

"What's going on with you?" Tracy asked. "How is your investigation going?"

She hadn't told anyone in her life, not even Tracy, about finding the stash in her mother's belongings and learning she'd been abandoned as an infant, or about her search to find her heritage. It was a secret she'd carried alone. Instead, she'd told her friends only that she was taking some time off to investigate a cold case that might make a good segment for her show. She also might have let them believe she needed some time to herself after her breakup with Jason. It was as good an excuse as any.

"Everything is fine. I'm not making as much progress as I'd hoped, but I have met some—" she thought about Quinn and smiled "—interesting people."

"Ooh, do tell. Anyone tall, dark and handsome?"

Again, Quinn's image popped into her mind. She hesitated a moment too long on his image and Tracy squealed. "You did meet someone, didn't you? Tell me everything."

"His name is Quinn Dawson. He's a reserve deputy with the local sheriff's office. He's very nice." He was also a mystery she would love to get to know better.

"A reserve deputy, huh? What does he do the rest of the time?"

"Private security, I think. He's obviously former military, but he's weirdly secretive about it."

"That sound ominous. Do I need to run a background on this new guy?"

Her friend was just being overprotective, knowing how Jason had broken her heart. "No, it's fine. We only met two days ago. That's not quite time enough to reveal deepest, darkest secrets to one another." But she had, in fact, revealed her deepest, darkest secret to him.

"I should try to get some sleep," she finally told Tracy.

"Maybe tomorrow will be a better day," her friend said and she couldn't agree more with the sentiment.

After all, it couldn't get any worse...unless she was killed.

Quinn hung up the phone at his desk in the sheriff's office and rubbed a weary hand over his face. He'd had a busy night following up on Rich's stalker theory. He'd talked to the local precinct in Chicago, the head of security at the studio where Dana worked and even with her producer at the television station. He'd found no evidence of threatening letters, phone calls, or inappropriate communication to Dana that might signal she had a stalker. It looked like the stalker theory was a dead end. Whatever these threats were about, they'd originated in West Bend.

He rocked backward in his chair as he ran through what he knew for the umpteenth time. Someone in his city wanted Dana to stop looking in to things that weren't her business, but all she was investigating was the Renfield murders. Was it really possible that after thirty years someone in town had something to hide about that night?

He sat up straight and keyed the name *Renfield* into the database on his computer. It was time he took a closer look at that case. Maybe it had nothing at all to do with Dana's attacks, but he wasn't going to leave any stone unturned until he found out who was threatening her and why. A message popped up alerting him that a digital file on the Renfield case wasn't available. He'd have to pull the paper file. He jotted down the case number, then glanced at the time on his phone and realized it was after 1:00 a.m. No one would be in the records department until Beverly Shorter, the documents clerk, arrived at seven. He could ask the deputy in charge to be let in, but since it wasn't an active case, Quinn doubted he would approve it. Besides, a thirty-year-old case file would likely be boxed up in storage. No, he would have to wait until Beverly arrived in the morning to help him find it.

He shut down his computer then headed home. He had time to catch a few hours of sleep, shower and shave, and return by the time Beverly showed up for work.

She was already there when he got back to the station and walked downstairs to the records room. He'd needed those few hours of sleep but couldn't wait to get his hands on the Renfield file.

She greeted him with a smile. "Good morning, Quinn. What can I help you with today?"

He'd known Beverly Shorter all his life. She'd been the file clerk in this office since his grandfather's time. "I need you to pull a file for me." He handed her the slip with the case number.

"Sure thing, hon. How's your mom doing?"

"She's doing good."

Beverly frowned at her computer. "Oh, dear, there's a flag on this file." She slipped the paper with the case number back to him. "I'm afraid I can't help you. Your father has to approve all requests to see this file."

The sheriff had to approve someone looking at a thirty-year-old case file? That seemed odd. Quinn wondered if Dana's visit to the precinct had anything to do with it. "When was that case flagged, Beverly?" he asked, fully expecting her to give yesterday's date.

"Looks like almost eleven years ago. Practically since the first day your father took office. I'll need his approval to release it."

Quinn was stunned by this new development. Why had his father flagged that file all those years ago? If it had been yesterday, he might understand, but eleven years earlier? What did that mean?

"I'll be back," he told her, then walked upstairs.

He knocked on his dad's office door then poked his head inside when his father's commanding voice shouted, "Enter."

"Do you have a minute?" Quinn asked him.

He turned from his computer. "Sure, what is it?"

"I need your approval to pull this case file."

His father took the number and typed it into the computer. He frowned when he saw which case Quinn wanted. "Why are you trying to pull the Renfield case? Does this have to do with that reporter?"

"She's been threatened and attacked multiple times already. I can't find any evidence that this was occurring before she came to town and the Renfield case is the only one she's looking in to. I thought I might find some connection if I examined the file."

"You won't find what you need in there."

"How do you know I won't?"

"Trust me, I know. There's nothing in that file that's going to lead you anywhere."

"I still want to see it for myself."

His father sighed, then picked up the handset of his desk phone and dialed an extension. "Beverly, will you bring me the Renfield file, please? Thank you." He hung up and glanced at Quinn. "Are you sure you want to go down this road?"

"Someone's after her. I can't sit back and do nothing."

"Your brother tells me you've been spending an awful lot of time with that reporter. That's not wise, Quinn."

He scrubbed a hand over his face. "I know." He didn't need to be reminded that he was flirting with danger. But he couldn't let her deal with this alone. What if the next time her attacker came, it was to do more than just threaten her? "She's all alone here. I know what that feels like."

His father stood and touched Quinn's shoulder. "Son, you've never been alone here."

Physically, his father was right. He had family surrounding him, there for him whenever he needed, but none of them had a clue what he'd been through. They didn't know how to relate to his experiences of fighting for his life or losing his best friend.

Beverly knocked on the door and walked inside, file in hand. "Here you go. This is all we have on the Renfield case."

She handed it to the sheriff, who passed it to Quinn. He took it, noting how thin it seemed. He opened it, expecting notes, photos, forensic reports. Instead, it was empty.

He glanced at his father, then at Beverly. "Is this a joke? Where is the file?"

His father nodded at Beverly that it was okay to leave. When the door closed behind her, he returned to his desk and sat down. "It's missing. We don't know what happened to it. All the evidence is gone, too. My first day in office, I pulled that file. It was like that then."

Quinn was outraged. "How could this happen? There must have been a ton of evidence and reports collected. There had to have been more than this."

"I'm sure there was, but it's all gone now. I don't know who did it or why, but it's gone."

He looked at his father, curiosity piquing his interest. "Why did you pull that file when you took office?"

His dad leaned across the desk and sighed. "Because Paul Renfield was my friend and I never in my heart truly believed he could do something so heinous. I wanted to see the evidence, examine it piece by piece, and decide for myself if he was guilty. I want to believe that file was misplaced and the evidence was lost accidentally. This case hit many people personally. I can see how papers could get scattered after being examined by numerous eyes, but everything? That's difficult for me to believe."

"You suspect someone intentionally destroyed that file?"

"I don't know, Quinn. I just don't know."

"Is that what Grandpa thought, too? He never discussed the case with me." Now Quinn wished he'd pressed his grandfather for more information about the case that had haunted him, but each time he'd asked about it, his grandfather had steered the conversation elsewhere. He'd always assumed it was to protect Quinn from the horror of knowing the realities of life and death, but now Quinn wondered if it wasn't more than that. Had he also been protecting himself from something he'd done?

"Your grandfather never discussed the case with me, but I know the files were there when he was in office. I saw him with them. I looked through them myself then, but I was only a young deputy and other, more senior investigators were handling the case."

Quinn left his father's office, feeling discouraged and confused. Why would someone want to remove all the information from the case file? It didn't make any sense. How would the case ever be solved or prosecuted now, assuming the perpetrator was found?

He walked outside but didn't head for his truck. He needed to walk to clear his mind so he could process what he'd just learned. It didn't make sense. Had those files accidentally been tossed out? Or had it been a deliberate act to cover up something that someone didn't want known?

Quinn glanced around at the shops on the square.

He'd always considered his hometown a safe haven. Sure, they had crime like any community did, but nothing like he'd seen in other towns, other places around the world. He wanted to believe this was all one big error and the rest of the file had been lost accidentally during a purge, or mixed in with another case in error. But his gut was telling him this was all connected. The missing pages. The threats against Dana. The attacks at the hotel, library and hospital. Someone in his town didn't want Dana Lang digging in to the Renfield case and they were taking measures to make sure she didn't.

He headed back to the department to pick up his truck, and dialed Dana's cell phone as he walked. "Meet me in front of the hotel in ten minutes.

Thankfully, she didn't ask questions until she was inside the pickup, buckling her seat belt.

"Where are we going? You sounded kind of jumpy on the phone."

"There's a secret compartment in the attic space of the shed behind my house. I remember peeking in through the window one time and seeing my grandfather put something up there. He tried to play it off like it wasn't a big deal, but I've always remembered it. I don't know why I never thought to look to see what he'd placed there. I inherited the house from him when he died. If he kept notes on the Renfield case, they'll be there."

She sucked in a breath, then smiled. "And you're going to share those with me? Quinn, that's wonderful. Thank you." She leaned across the seat and threw her arms around him, pulling him into a hug. She'd caught him off guard in this embrace, but he enjoyed the feel of her in his arms. It had been a long time since he'd been this close to a woman.

She must have sensed his hesitation because she pulled away from him and quickly apologized. "I'm sorry. I shouldn't have done that. It was inappropriate."

"It's fine," he told her, trying to calm the racing of his pulse. He quickly started the engine and drove toward his home.

"What changed your mind?" she asked as he drove.

He turned and tried to focus his attention back on the case and on the road ahead of him. "I got a look at the case file. My father had a good reason for not letting you see it. It's gone."

"What's gone?"

"Everything. Everything is missing."

"How does that happen?"

"Who knows. I spoke to my father. He said the file was that way when he took office. There were eight years between the time my grandfather died and my dad took office. It could have happened during that time…but then again, I suppose it could have happened any time before that. My dad flagged that file so he would know when someone was trying to look at it. I don't know if my grandpa took any precautions like that or not."

She sat back in her seat, her face showing her disappointment and confusion, just as he'd felt earlier. "All the evidence they collected—"

"Gone."

She glanced at him. "You're thinking your grandfather has copies, aren't you? I hope he did."

"Yeah, me, too."

"Does this mean you're finally coming around to believing this all has something to do with the Renfield case?"

"All I know, Dana, is that someone is targeting you and right now following this trail is the best lead we have to discover who it is."

She reached out and took his hand, smiling at him with grateful eyes. "Thank you for including me in this. You didn't have to."

He realized he hadn't even thought about excluding her. He made up his mind to dig through those files and immediately thought of her. It was an odd but comforting realization. As much as he'd planned to keep his distance, he didn't want to. He was drawn to her, and it was more than the softness of her skin or the way she smelled like jasmine. It was her spunk and passion for discovering the truth that attracted him.

He started to tell her not to worry, but his words were halted when he spotted something racing toward them in his review mirror. His eyes moved to the side mirror. The car was on their bumper now and he could tell it was a sports car of some kind. Judging by the grill, an older version Charger.

"I think we have company," he said, gripping the

steering wheel even harder and bracing himself for a confrontation of some kind. He didn't recognize the vehicle and this stretch of road didn't get much through traffic.

Please, Lord, let them be lost tourists.

He slowed down, hoping the car would go around them. Instead, it remained on their bumper for several more moments. Dana was silent on the seat beside him. He didn't even have to look at her to know she was on alert just as he was.

The car swerved into the oncoming lane as if to pass them. The passenger-side window came down and a figure leaned out. Quinn's gut clenched when he saw the mask covering the man's face. He slammed on the gas as the figure produced a rifle and aimed it their way.

"Get down!" Quinn hollered as the shot rang out, hitting the back of his truck's bed. He grabbed Dana and pushed her to the seat. "Get your head down."

"What's happening?" she asked. "Who are they?"

He gripped the steering wheel and kicked into survival mode, swerving on the road to make them more difficult to hit. He glanced out the mirror and saw both the driver and passenger were wearing masks to hide their faces. Another shot rang out, this one hitting the back window. It shattered and sprayed the front seat. "I wish I knew."

Dana screamed and covered her head with her hands as she crouched by the seat as best she could while wearing her seat belt. He nearly told her to remove it so she could slide to the floor, but he wasn't entirely sure he could keep them on the road and she might need it if he couldn't.

Another shot rang out. This one hit a tire. Quinn heard the pop of the rubber blow, then the truck veered sharply to the right, sending them spinning. He turned into the spin, doing his best to right the vehicle, but the truck was going too fast.

"Hang on," he shouted before the truck smashed into the guardrail and tilted into the air. His seat belt locked as he was thrown forward, and he heard Dana scream as the truck plummeted down the embankment, rolling with each sickening turn.

FOUR

Pain shot through Dana as the truck slammed to a stop at the bottom of the embankment. Every muscle in her body ached and the sudden jarring of the crash disoriented her. She groaned and reached to unlock the seat belt. She was thankful for the safety feature that had kept her from going through the windshield, but she was upside down and ready for the world to stop turning. She managed to find the button and press it, falling onto the roof of the cab now beneath her feet.

Beside her, Quinn groaned, his shock at being jarred obviously beginning to wear off. He was no longer in his seat but was sprawled on the upside-down roof. She saw his seat belt had snapped at some point and sent him reeling. He'd sustained a gash on his head that was bleeding profusely and his legs were trapped under the dash, which had fallen on top of him during the tumble.

She stumbled toward him. "Can you pull yourself free?"

He tried one then the other, grimacing in pain with the right. "I can't. Even if I could, I think my ankle might be broken." He glanced around the cab. "Where's my cell phone? Do you see it?"

She glanced around the mess that was now the ceiling of the cab and spotted his phone. It was crushed. She picked it up and showed it to him.

"What about yours? Is it still working?"

Hers had been damaged in her fall down the stairs, but it had still worked. When she found it this time, though, it was damaged beyond repair. She shook her head at him, his face as grim as she felt at this moment.

"Do you have GPS assistance?"

"No, this truck is too old for it to have come pre-installed and I never thought I would need to add it since I only use it when I'm in town." He pushed himself up. "Look behind the seat. My rifle should be back there somewhere."

She found the rifle beneath what remained of the back seat. She handed it to him and he checked it. "It doesn't look damaged and it's loaded." He pushed it into her hands. "Now take it and go for help."

She realized his meaning and thrust it back to him. "I'm not leaving you."

"You have to. There's no way I can make it on this ankle and whoever it was that ran us off the road will be coming back to make sure we're dead. You have to go now. My parents' house is only a mile through the woods. It's the closest place around. You can call for help."

She was torn with the decision of what to do. She couldn't leave Quinn, but they had no phone, no GPS and no other way of getting help if she didn't. He was right about those guys coming back. This had been no mere threat on her life. They'd been shooting with purpose. But if she left, would she come back to find Quinn dead? She couldn't deal with that.

"I'm not leaving you," she insisted, moving to try to pull on the dashboard enough to free his legs.

"Dana, stop. You have to go."

"I said I'm not leaving you." She pulled at the dashboard again, pressing her weight into it, and nearly fell backward when it moved. She glanced back to Quinn.

"I think you got it," he said. He wriggled his leg until his left foot slipped through. Unfortunately, his right foot remained wedged beneath the dash. "I can't get it free," he said after several attempts. "It's just not coming."

She tried again, pushing and pulling and putting her weight against the solid material. He used his left foot to aid her, trying to gain some leverage against the heavy object.

Finally, she stopped to catch her breath. It wasn't budging.

He sat up suddenly and looked through the window, then grabbed her arm. "Dana, they're here. You have to run. Go through the woods. Get help. Even if I could get free, I can't outrun them. You can."

She shook her head fiercely. "No, I'm not leaving you."

He picked up the rifle and pressed it into her hands. "You don't have a choice. Now go."

She heard the squeal of tires above them and knew the men had returned, but how could she leave him stranded and trapped with no way to defend himself? She couldn't. She wouldn't.

She pushed the gun back to him, making her decision. "I'll go, but you keep this. You'll need it."

"No, you will. You're the one they're coming after."

"Yes, but I'll have the woods to shield me and a head start. You need this to protect yourself." She jutted out her chin. "Otherwise, we both stay."

He grunted with irritation, but took the rifle from her hand. "Go. Head into the woods. You'll come across a creek. Follow it upstream a half mile and you'll see my parents' farm. If they're not there, break a window and use the phone to call for help."

She nodded, taking in the directions. But there was one thing she needed to do before she left him— something she couldn't leave without doing if this might be the last time she ever saw him alive.

She leaned in and touched his lips with hers. Tears pressed her eyes. She didn't want to leave him here alone. She wanted to bask in his presence and let the feel of his arms around her lure her into a happy safety. But she couldn't stay and they both knew it. "Not goodbye," she whispered to him. "Just in case."

His face was flushed but she couldn't tell if it was from the kiss or the pain wrenching his leg. "Go," he said. "Don't let them find you."

She crawled through the broken window shards of the side glass and glanced around. They were at the bottom of a gulley. Climbing the hill and flagging down a car might be easier, but she hadn't seen that many cars on this road and the men who'd shot at them were now at the top. She could hear them talking, but she couldn't make out their conversation. She wasn't sticking around to find out, either. Quinn was right to send her through the woods. She only wished she wasn't so afraid of what lurked out there.

She leaned down to see him sitting against the outline of the cab. "I'll be back for you," she promised. It was a promise she intended on keeping.

Please keep him safe, she prayed to God, hoping for once He would listen to her.

Then she took a deep breath and entered the brush.

The pain in his leg was excruciating. Quinn tried to pull his leg free but still couldn't. He was glad Dana was gone, but he hoped she wouldn't take too long to bring help. He was certain the men who'd run them off the road would soon be coming down to make sure they were both dead.

A noise outside the truck grabbed his attention. He clutched the rifle and tried to turn so he'd have a better position from which to shoot anyone who came for him. Sweat poured down his forehead and pain ripped through his leg as he moved. He tried to slow down his racing pulse and listen. He heard someone out there, the faint sound barely reaching his ears.

He scanned the area he could see outside the truck, but it was mostly blocked by the overturned vehicle.

His thoughts kept returning to Dana. Had it been the right call to send her into the woods? It didn't matter. It had been the only thing he could do. If she'd stayed here with him, she would have been a sitting target.

The memory of that kiss floated into his mind and he pushed it back, as far back as he could send it. It had been a warm and glorious moment that had sent his blood pressure spiking with enjoyment, but focusing on that now meant certain danger for him. He had to keep his mind on the current situation and not the one he wanted to repeat very soon…if he made it out of this alive.

He leaned into his weapon as the sound of footsteps neared him. Arching to listen for a second set of steps, he heard only one. Better for him. Not so good for Dana. That meant she was in more trouble than he'd hoped. Two men had been inside the car. One driving, the other shooting out the window. Where was the other guy? Was he somewhere Quinn couldn't see him? Or was he after Dana?

His stomach clenched, and he prayed that wasn't so. They wouldn't know yet that she was gone and he intended to keep that information to himself for as long as possible.

He slid the safety back carefully, quietly. It wasn't the first time he'd been trapped and had to rely on his instincts and his training for responses. Second-guessing himself never worked. He'd been trained to handle situations like this both during his time with Delta and in his covert security work.

He had to be careful, though. He couldn't assume this was one of the men who'd attacked them. This could simply be some hunter walking through the woods who'd come upon the overturned vehicle. He had to wait until the man showed himself and his true intent.

He held his breath while the man approached. His steps were cautious and slow. Quinn waited for the man to lower himself. *Please let it be a friendly face*, he prayed, but he prepared for the worst.

He knew which way this was going when he heard the click of a safety being removed. He took aim and fired his rifle, hitting the man first in the leg then with another shot to the stomach as he fell. Bullets sprayed the cab as the man returned fire even as he hit the ground. Quinn dropped the rifle and lowered his head. He couldn't move but he took as much cover from the old pickup as its battered and crashed body would allow. When it was over and he realized he wasn't hit, he sent praise toward heaven. Only God could have gotten him through that without a scratch. He scooped up the rifle and readied it again, but the man on the ground outside his window didn't reach for his weapon, which had slipped to the ground. Quinn watched him, but he didn't move to get up, even though Quinn could clearly see the man was still breathing. In fact, he looked to be gasping for air.

Somehow in all the commotion and bullet fire, the

truck had shifted and Quinn's leg slipped out from beneath the dash. It hurt like crazy, but he wasn't sure anymore it was broken. He could deal with the pain, but if it was broken it wouldn't support his weight.

He crawled out of the cab and pulled himself to his feet. The man he'd shot was lying on the ground a few feet away. His breathing was heavy and Quinn knew even from this distance that he was dying. He'd watched Tommy go the same way, gasping for each and every breath through the blood pooling into his lungs and knowing each one could be his last. There was nothing Quinn could do to help this man, and he also didn't pose any further threat. His time left on this earth was nearly done.

Quinn carefully placed weight on his ankle and his foot didn't buckle. That was good news. It meant he could at least hobble away instead of being a sitting target for this guy's partner.

He walked to the man on the ground, checked the guy's pockets and found his wallet. His identification listed him as Clifford Lincoln. He didn't know the name and he didn't recognize the guy, either.

"Why did you come after us?" he demanded.

The man's grey eyes looked at him, but he couldn't speak.

Whoever he was, Quinn doubted he had anything to do with the Renfield case. He didn't look older than twenty-five or twenty-six. Not even born when the murders occurred. "What did you want with us? Did someone hire you to kill us?"

The man's eyes glazed over and he died without answering a single question.

Quinn picked up the guy's gun and tucked it into his pocket. He still had his rifle and didn't know if he would need the extra weapon, but he was taking it just in case. He wasn't going to take a shot in the back because he'd failed to commandeer a dead man's gun that someone else had picked up.

Quinn glanced at the path Dana had taken into the woods. If she'd made it to his parents' house then help should be on the way soon. He debated whether to follow and try to catch up with her, or climb the embankment and wait on them to arrive.

After testing his ankle, he decided to wait it out. He wanted to be at the top of the embankment, though, so he'd use his upper body strength and his good leg to pull himself to the top.

However, movement at the top stopped him. He hobbled to the trees and stood waiting and watching as another man climbed down the embankment.

"Cliff? What's taking so long," the man called as he descended. "I heard the shots five minutes ago."

He landed on his feet and headed for the truck. Quinn backed farther into the brush, doing his best to disappear into the trees. He released the safety of the gun as he watched the man kneel over his friend's dead body. His mask was on his head but not pulled down over his face, and Quinn got a good look at the man. Like Clifford Lincoln, this guy was too young to have been alive when the Renfield murders occurred. He looked to be no older than twenty-four.

He was tall and lanky, just like the man who'd broken into Dana's hotel room and attacked her at the hospital, and his hair was blond with a tinge of red.

He swore, then jumped to his feet and pulled a gun. Marching to the truck, the man looked inside, then scanned the woods. But Quinn knew how to blend in and he was certain the man didn't see him. He did, however, see the path Dana had made into the woods and headed that way.

A cell phone rang and the man pulled it from his pocket and answered it. "No, it's not done. Cliff is dead. I know you wanted it to look like a car accident, but they didn't die in the crash. I think they ran into the woods." He paused a moment, then nodded. "I understand. Yes, I'll handle it." He ended the call and slid his phone back into his pocket. "Fine. I'll kill her myself," he muttered, then headed into the brush.

"No, you won't," Quinn whispered as he followed the gunman into the woods, grimacing with each painful step. He'd sent Dana off alone and he was going to make sure this guy didn't track her down, even if he had to crawl on his hands and knees to get it done. Then he was going to get his hands on that phone and find out the reason whoever had been on the other end of that call wanted her dead.

Dana pushed past brush and limbs as she made her way through the woods. Tears slid down her face and she let them come. She wished Quinn was here with her now. She worried about him alone and trapped. She'd heard gunshots earlier that had star-

tled her, but she couldn't concentrate on the ramifi-
cations of it. She'd left him the rifle for protection,
and if she'd learned anything about him, it was that
he could take care of himself. She had to believe that.

But she still had to continue on as if someone
was chasing her even if she didn't know for certain.
She'd heard gunshots and there had been two men
in the car. Was it possible Quinn had taken them
both out? It seemed unlikely, which was the reason
for the tears. But she couldn't think about that now.
She had to keep going. She couldn't quit.

The leaves crunched beneath her feet, causing
her to grimace. Would the sound give her away to
whoever was chasing her? Sunlight burst through
the overhanging limbs, bathing certain sections in
light and casting shadows in others—where a killer
could hide in plain sight. The scent of the pine trees
was overwhelming and every so often she froze in
fear when the scuttling of some animal grabbed her
attention. She felt her heart flutter with every sound,
as she was uncertain what caused it or if it meant she
was being followed.

Limbs clawed at her face and arms and legs, and
her heels sunk into the soft dirt. If only she'd worn
sneakers or boots today, but here she was traipsing
through the woods in her high heels.

She stopped and glanced at a tree with a distinc-
tive root section. Hadn't she seen that one before?
Fear wrapped around her, sucking all the oxygen
from her lungs. Was she walking in circles? She.
Just. Didn't. Know.

She picked up two sticks and placed one on top of the other in an *X* shape. Now she would know for certain if she passed this tree again and if she was walking in circles. She kept going, navigating the leaf-lined ground.

She trudged on, needing to reach help. The sound of voices caught on the wind and she stopped to listen, hoping against hope it wasn't the men coming after her. But it was definitely someone speaking. She couldn't understand who was talking or where the sound was coming from, but she knew someone was close by. Was it the men chasing her? Or someone who would help? She longed to call out for help, but could she risk it?

She stopped, leaned against a tree and let the tears flow freely. She was scared and lost and by herself. She'd never felt as alone as she did now in these woods. She stared up through the trees to the clear blue sky overhead and suddenly the urge to pray overwhelmed her. She wanted to. She truly did. But God was the one that had placed her in this situation. He'd abandoned her a long time ago, just as everyone else in her life had, and she was through begging Him for help.

She jerked her head toward a sound that caught her ear. Footsteps. Someone was approaching.

She ran to hide behind a tree large enough to camouflage her. When she did, she saw the trampled limbs and brush and realized she'd been leaving an obvious trail behind her as she trudged through the woods. She'd left a path for the killers to follow.

She stood straight and kept still as a figure appeared from the brush. She wished it was Quinn and that he'd somehow freed himself and come to find her. She held her breath as a figure moved to where she could see him. Disappointment filled her as she spotted a man enter the clearing. He was dressed in jeans, a denim jacket, a button-up shirt and sneakers, an indication that he surely wasn't a hunter in the woods. He'd come here for one purpose—to kill her.

Another thought pulsed through her. If he was here, then where was Quinn? Did that mean Quinn was dead?

She remained still as he stopped to survey the area. She hadn't continued on, so the brush wasn't tamped down anywhere. He turned and scoped out the area. She held her breath again as his eyes roamed over the trees. She was thankful for the protection of the tree, but she knew it wasn't too far-fetched for him to realize where she was hiding.

His gaze zeroed in on where she was hiding. She closed her eyes, hoping he hadn't noticed her, but when she heard him move her way, she knew she was found. She opened her eyes to see him lifting a gun in her direction.

She screamed and took off running. He fired off several shots that hit the ground near her. Finally, he rushed to her and grabbed her by the hair, pulling her back before she could escape.

"Got you!" he cried.

She clutched his hands as he pulled her to the ground. She couldn't loosen them. When he let go and kneeled beside her, she struggled to get away from him. He grabbed her arms and pinned her down with his knees.

"That's enough," he said. "No one's here to save you now."

Fear burst through her. This man was going to kill her, but she wasn't ready to die. She struggled with him but was easily overpowered. He was tall and thin but stronger than her and it would take extreme measures for her to get free. But she had to keep fighting. She wouldn't give up. Her only hope was to continue struggling and hope she was able to wriggle free and grab something to use as a weapon.

A gun fired, startling both of them. A moment later, he fell to the ground holding his shoulder. Dana scrambled to her feet and grabbed a sturdy limb to fight him off and only then noticed blood oozing onto his shirt sleeve.

Behind her, another sound grabbed her attention. She spun around, holding the limb as a weapon as someone emerged from the brush.

"Dana, it's me" the man said, and when Dana heard his voice she melted into tears.

Quinn! He was alive!

Behind her, the man who'd attacked her scrambled to his feet and took off through the woods.

Quinn leaned against a tree for support. Only then did she remember his injured foot. He was in no position to chase down an attacker. She was thankful he'd made it this far to help her when she'd needed it.

She tossed down the branch and walked to him. "Are you okay? How's your ankle?"

"Not broken, so that's good."

"What do we do now?"

He was growing pale and she suspected he was in more pain than he wanted her to know. "We continue on. My parents' house isn't far."

He pushed off and started to walk, but grimaced and slid back against the tree.

"It's okay," she said, touching his arm. "I'll help you."

Dana slipped his arm across her shoulder and acted as a support for him. He leaned into her and limped along. It wasn't ideal, but she wasn't leaving his side again until they were out of these woods and out of danger.

They weren't very far when he stopped, stood straight and picked up the rifle, aiming it toward the trees in front of them. Then she heard it, too. The rustling of leaves as someone moved through the woods. She remained beside him, ready to fight if necessary as the sound grew louder. Someone was heading right toward them.

She held her breath as Quinn tensed. He was ready.

"Quinn," a voice called and she felt him immediately relax.

He lowered the weapon. "Over here," he shouted in return, then put his arm back over Dana's shoulder and leaned into her.

Two figures emerged from the brush and she saw it was John and Rich Dawson. Quinn's father and brother.

"I came home for lunch and Rich joined me. We heard shots fired and saw the truck off the road," John stated. "What happened?"

"We were run off the road, then someone chased us through the woods." He handed his dad the rifle. "I killed one of them."

"What about the others. Are they still out here?"

"I shot the other one in the shoulder while he was attacking Dana. He ran into the woods that way," he said, indicating the direction the attacker had fled.

"Are you hurt?" Rich asked, noticing how he was leaning on Dana.

"When the truck flipped, my foot was caught. I don't think it's broken but it hurts like you wouldn't believe."

"Let's get you both to the hospital, then we'll talk in detail," Rich said, moving to his brother and allowing him to lean on him instead.

Dana was glad not to have to bear his weight, but she found she missed having him close. She felt exposed and alone as he hobbled off with Rich. She glanced at John, who led her out of the woods.

"Can you at least give a description of the guy this time?" he asked her as they walked.

"Absolutely, I can." This guy had messed up big-time now. She'd seen his face and she would never forget it.

Dana chewed on her fingernail as she sat anxiously in the hospital waiting room. She'd already given her statement to Quinn's dad in the car on the way to there. He'd promised to update her on Quinn's condition when he knew something. That had been over an hour ago.

Finally, the doors opened and Sheriff Dawson and a nice-looking woman about his age wearing slacks and a blouse entered.

Dana jumped up as they approached her. "How's Quinn?"

Sheriff Dawson answered. "He'll be fine. The X-rays showed no breaks."

She breathed a sigh of relief. "That's good."

"We identified the first man Quinn shot. His name was Clifford Lincoln. Does that name sound familiar to you?"

She shook her head. "I don't recognize it. Who is he?"

"A local man known to be a drug addict. He was twenty-three and already had four arrests for drug possession under his belt."

"Twenty-three? How could he be involved with this? He wasn't even born thirty years ago." Why then was this man after her?

"He may have been a hired gun. We need to identify the other guy he was with. Did you recognize him?"

"No, although he did remind me of the man who broke into my hotel room."

"Quinn gave me a description. We're going to circulate it and we'll need both of you to work with a sketch artist."

"No problem." She recalled his dark beady eyes

as they scanned the woods searching for her. She didn't even know what she'd done to deserve such animosity from him.

"Now that we have an identification on the dead guy, we'll check his known associates to see if we can find anyone who matches that description or anything that might lead us to why he was involved in this. We're also checking his financials to see if we can uncover any new deposits into his accounts that might lead us back to whomever hired him." He turned to the woman beside him. "I'm going back to the station. They should have Quinn's truck towed in by now. I want to see what kind of evidence might show up."

The woman held out her hand to Dana to shake. "I'm sorry for my husband's manners. He seems to have forgotten to introduce me. I'm Clara Dawson, Quinn's mother."

Bill Mackey's daughter. Dana longed to ask her about her father, things that only a daughter might know, like was her father the type of person to abandon a child? But now wasn't the time. "It's nice to meet you, Mrs. Dawson."

She waved away the formalities. "It's Clara, please. Nice to meet you, too."

Dana was surprised by the anger that crept up inside of her when she thought about what this woman's father had done to her. She'd been abandoned. Sure, it might have been to protect her, but how could abandoning a child count as protection? He'd been a sheriff, for crying out loud. He could have protected her himself. She hadn't even realized how angry she was about that until just this moment, but she was. She wanted answers, but the man who could give them was no longer around and his daughter wasn't to blame for what he'd done.

She gave Dana a big smile. "You're much prettier in person than you are on TV."

"Thank you. You're very kind."

She turned to her husband. "We'll be fine," she said and he nodded.

"I'll go check in at the office then." He kissed Clara, then walked out.

"I'm sorry this happened to Quinn," Dana told her. "I'm sure it's because of me, because of my investigation into the Renfield murders. Someone is targeting me."

Clara took the seat beside Dana. "John told me you were looking in to the Renfield murders. Are you doing a story on it?"

Dana started to give her the official spiel, but stopped. This was Quinn's mother and he might have already told them the truth about her. "No, this is personal. My mother died a little while ago and I recently learned that not only was I adopted, but I was also abandoned at a church not far from here. She had a newspaper article about the Renfield murders, a letter from the preacher who I was left with and a handwritten note from the person who'd left me." She waited to see the woman's reaction, but she didn't seem to be putting the pieces together.

"I don't understand."

"I have reason to believe Alicia Renfield didn't

die that night. In fact, I believe I'm Alicia Renfield. That's why I'm in town, to investigate that possibility."

Clara Dawson gave her a skeptical look. "That's not possible. The baby died in the fire. Everyone knows that." She looked at Dana, seeming to study her face, then sucked in a breath. She reached out a hand and touched Dana's chin, lifting it to get a better look at her. "I knew Rene. You do have the same strong jaw and sharp features."

Dana felt her heart rise. Someone who'd known Rene said she looked like her. This was the most encouragement she'd had since she'd started this journey.

"I realize this is all very shocking, but I was found with a handwritten note. Quinn saw it and said it looked like your father's writing. Do you think he would…?" Suddenly she realized she couldn't say the words "abandon a child." But he had. He had abandoned her in the cold, harsh world.

Clara seemed to understand her intention without offense. "No, he wouldn't. If he left Alicia—you—there, he would have made certain someone took you in or he had another plan in place. He wouldn't just abandon a child."

"Why do you think he would do that in the first place?"

"I don't know. It must have been something very serious, though. He and my mother used to babysit Alicia. Rene's parents died years ago and she had no one else. They loved that little girl as if she was their own grandchild. I find it hard to believe he would let her go without good reason. I always thought his reaction to her death was odd. He never cried, and from that day on he was much more stoic than he had been. I thought it was the grief of losing her, of not being able to save her. I remember being glad that Paul's parents weren't around to see this happen. It would have devastated them."

"Do you think Paul did it? Killed Rene, I mean?"

Dana could see the struggle in Clara's face. "I just don't know," she finally stated. "I know he loved her. No one knows better than me, the daughter and wife of a cop, that things happen between a husband and wife you'd never expect, but I never would have thought Paul was the kind of man who would flee if something had happened. That's always bothered me."

Dana had heard that sentiment before during her time investigating cold cases as part of her news program. "I suppose it goes to show that you never truly know how someone will react to a situation."

Clara nodded. "Yes, you're right about that."

The double doors opened and a nurse appeared and told them they could go back to see Quinn.

Clara motioned to her. "Why don't you go in first. He was asking for you earlier, wanting to know that you were okay. It'll do him good to see you're not hurt."

She thanked Clara, then followed the nurse down the hall to a room. She entered and saw Quinn lying on the bed, his foot propped up on a pillow.

A grin spread across his face when he spotted her. "Dana, come in. I'm glad to see you're okay."

"I'm fine." She walked to his bedside and he took her hand. "I was worried about you."

"I should be worried about you, not the other way around." He smiled, a nice big smile. He squeezed her hand firmly.

Suddenly, she recalled the kiss she'd given him in the truck. Was he remembering that and thinking it meant more than it did. And who was she kidding? She liked Quinn, liked the way he thought about her and tried to act protective. And she liked the way he stood up for what he believed, including telling her like it was when needed. She squeezed his hand back.

"When are you getting out of here?"

"Tonight. They're not keeping me. Why don't you come to my house tomorrow and we'll find those boxes and dig through Grandpa's notes?"

"Are you sure you're up for that?"

"The people who did this, they took it to a new level, Dana. They're not just threatening you anymore. This was an attempt to silence you by any means. I want to catch them."

She shuddered, realizing he was right. The thought of going back to her hotel room frightened her. Would they be waiting for her there to finish the job?

He must have seen the concern on her face because he pulled at her hand until she looked at him. "Hey, it's going to be okay. I've arranged to have a deputy drive you to the hotel and keep guard. My father approved protection for you tonight. You won't be alone."

She gave him a half smile. It seemed he could look right through her tough exterior to see the frightened little girl inside. How did he know she feared being alone? "You didn't have to do that," she insisted, but she was glad he had. Even from the hospital bed, he was doing everything in his power to protect her.

"Then I'll see you tomorrow." She stood, holding on to his hand until their distance caused it to slip from her grasp. She was saddened at the loss of his touch and that realization surprised her.

Oh, yes, she was definitely falling hard for this man.

Quinn didn't like the crutches he was forced to use just to get from the car to his house. He hadn't even wanted to come home, but Rich had refused to drive him to the hotel so he could make sure Dana was safe.

Rich followed behind him carrying a bag of his belongings from the hospital. He set it on the floor next to the couch, then handed Quinn a bottle of painkillers they'd stopped to get on their way home.

"Take these for the pain."

"I don't need them," he insisted. He didn't want to be drugged. He needed to be alert and on guard if today's events were any indication.

"Take them," Rich insisted. "You can't do anything to help Dana if you can't even walk. You should be thankful that ankle is only sprained and not broken. Take care of it tonight so you can be useful tomorrow."

He grabbed the bag with his belongings and dug through it. "Where's my cell phone?"

"It's toast," Rich said. "I'll get you a new one tomorrow."

"Loan me yours," Quinn said. Rich eyed him and Quinn knew his brother thought he was crazy, but he couldn't help himself. He needed to know she was okay and if he couldn't go see her, he was going to call. He wouldn't be able to rest until he made sure she was safe.

"She's fine, Quinn. I handled the protection assignments myself. Dougherty is going to stand guard tonight and Jenkins will take over in the morning."

"I just need to talk to her to make sure."

Finally, Rich handed over his phone and Quinn dialed the number for the hotel. Her cell phone was also broken beyond repair from the wreck, but he knew he could reach her through the hotel's phone. Milo was on duty at the front desk and he quickly rang Dana's room.

"Hello." Her wispy voice floated over him, and he realized he loved the sound of it.

"Hi there."

"Quinn, are you home?"

"I am. Just arrived. I wanted to make certain you were okay before I turned in for the night."

"Yes, I'm fine. I do feel better knowing there is someone standing watch outside the door. Thank your father and brother for me."

"I will."

"I'm just going over some notes. My producer has been blowing up my email with show prep."

After all she'd been through today, the wreck and nearly being killed, she was calmly doing work for her show. She had a way of compartmentalizing her emotions, which he liked. It was a trait he recognized from his time in Delta and in doing contract security for the CIA. There were jobs where no matter what was going on in your life, you had to put things aside and focus on what needed to be done. Few civilians understood that concept.

"Well, try to get some sleep. You've had a hard day and we're starting fresh tomorrow, remember?"

"I remember." The line went silent for a moment then she spoke again. "Are you sure you'll be up to it?"

"I've already told you I was."

"I know. I was making sure."

"We're going to figure this out, Dana. Everything's going to be fine. I promise."

There were so many things he wanted to say to her. How he'd been hurt but was ready to take another shot at being with someone. How her courage and determination impressed him more and more each day. He opened his mouth to say something, anything. Nothing came out, but he wasn't yet ready to break the connection between them.

But what was he thinking even going down this road with her? Her heart was for the story and his was the biggest story of all right now. The closer he got to her, the more likely she was to find out about his connection to Rizzo and the embassy attack.

God, why would You place someone like Dana in my path and expect me not to fall for her?

"I'll see you tomorrow," she said finally.

"Yeah, I'll see you," he told her, then listened as she hung up the phone.

When the line was silent, he handed the phone back to Rich, who took it and slipped it back into his pocket. Quinn rubbed a hand over his face.

Rich must have seen the emotions on his face. "What are you going to do?"

"I don't know." The truth was he was already more enamored of her than he had been of anyone in such a long time. His first thought was of her and seeing her smile and the cute way she cocked her head to the side when she was thinking.

"Maybe you should tell her the truth."

"I can't."

As much as he was growing to care for this woman, he didn't trust her and a relationship couldn't be built without trust. No, he would just have to learn to push aside his attraction for her and compartmentalize his feelings. It wouldn't be the first time he'd had to keep his emotions in check.

But it would definitely be the most difficult.

FIVE

Dana clicked the police station's computer mouse to move forward to the next group of photos. Sheriff Dawson had phoned her at the hotel that morning and asked her to come and look at mug shots to try to identity the man who had attacked her in the woods. The deputy on duty outside her door had driven her over and she'd already spent an hour clicking through photos without any success.

Rich walked over and took a seat across from her. "Find anything yet?"

"No, not yet. Have you seen Quinn today? How is he feeling?"

"I went by there earlier and took him a replacement cell phone. He said he was okay but I could tell he was in pain. They say it's always worse the next day."

She'd heard that, too, and she was definitely feeling more beaten up than yesterday from the truck flipping. And he'd been hurt worse than she'd been.

"We're supposed to meet up later today. Maybe I should cancel?"

"Nah, I wouldn't. I think it'll do him good to see you."

She was surprised to hear him say that. She was also surprised by the way her heart jumped to hear it. "Really?"

His face reddened. "Oh, boy. He'll kill me for saying that, but it's true." He leaned forward and looked at her. "My brother is really putting himself out there to help you. I hope he can trust you."

She liked the way this family looked out for one another and suddenly felt a pang of jealousy. Who did she have in her life that ever had her back that way? "I appreciate what Quinn is doing for me. I wouldn't do anything to purposefully hurt him."

"I hope not." He got up to leave and she turned back to the computer. She clicked the mouse again and another page of mug shots appeared on the screen. She gasped when she spotted a familiar face among them.

"This is him," she cried, causing Rich to turn back to her. She pointed to a man with a thin face and reddish blond hair. "That's definitely the man that attacked me in the woods."

"Are you sure?"

"Absolutely. I doubt I'll ever forget that face. Who is he?"

"Reed Jessup."

"Jessup? I've heard that name before but I can't recall where."

"He's Mayor Jessup's nephew. The mayor and his wife practically raised Reed. He's also a known drug addict arrested multiple times, but because of his family's connections, the charges never stick. Usually, whenever he gets into real trouble, they ship him off to rehab."

She had never met Mayor Jessup but perhaps she'd seen his name somewhere around town. "Why would he want to kill me?"

"I'm sure he doesn't. Quinn said he overheard a phone conversation in the woods that led him to believe someone paid those men to run you off the road. When we locate him, we can ask him who it was. I'll put out a BOLO for him. When are you going to see Quinn?"

"Not until this afternoon. First, I need to replace my cell phone, then I want to go back to the library and spend some more time on the microfiche."

"Okay. I'll phone him and catch him up on this new development. Deputy Jenkins will stay with you and drive you."

"I'm sure I'll be fine."

"Dana, my brother would hammer me if I let you leave here unprotected. Whoever paid Reed Jessup and Clifford Lincoln to run you off the road yesterday meant to kill you. Don't be reckless. Take the precaution and let us at the sheriff's office do our jobs and find this maniac before he tries again."

She liked Rich's bluntness. He didn't sugarcoat her situation and she appreciated it. It was a natural instinct for her to try to put on a brave face, but she was frightened. The man who'd attacked her in the woods—Reed Jessup—had shown up in her nightmares last night, making her rest uneasy.

She nodded, then stood. "Okay. I'll stay with Deputy Jenkins. Tell Quinn I'll see him later this afternoon."

She left the sheriff's office and made it to the library without incident, feeling a little conspicuous at having an armed escort follow her inside. She waved to Lila as she walked through the main room, then she went upstairs. The microfiche machine was still there waiting for her even though it had been two days since someone had lured her into the staircase. The mysterious Reed Jessup? Or his friend, whom Quinn had shot and killed? Hopefully, she would soon find out when the police apprehended Reed. But the real question was who was the person paying them to harm her? And why?

She sat down, pulled up the first microfiche and scanned through the newspaper copies. There had to be something she was missing, something that would help her prove she was Alicia Renfield and unmask whomever was behind all this. She couldn't wait to get her hands on those files of Quinn's grandfather. In the meantime, she would follow up every lead she could.

She went back over the days after the fire. Eventually the Renfield murders were relegated from the front page and placed further back in the paper until the mentions of the case stopped altogether.

She sighed. She had to be missing something.

She had to go back to the beginning, to the motive for the murders. She pulled out her notebook. There were only a handful of reasons people committed murder. Love and betrayal were the most obvious. The unofficial story, according to the newspaper articles, was that Paul had discovered Rene was going to run off with another man and he snapped and murdered his family. But had he meant to try to kill Alicia? Perhaps if he'd believed she wasn't his child, he might have wanted her dead. Whatever had happened, something had lead Sheriff Mackey to believe she had been a target. Otherwise, she wouldn't have needed to be hidden away as protection.

Greed didn't make sense, either. How would anyone profit from the deaths of Rene or Alicia? Was there a massive life insurance policy on them? And if so, who collected it? She could imagine a scenario where Rene was killed for whatever reason, but what kind of monster would have had the stomach to kill an infant? A very sick individual indeed. But if Alicia was believed to be dead then the killer or killers could profit from the insurance. She would assume Rene and Paul were beneficiaries for each other, but if Paul had been killed to collect the insurance money, why hadn't his body been left where it would be found? And who would collect on Rene and Alicia's insurance payout if Paul didn't? It was an avenue that deserved to be checked out. She added a note to check to see if there were any life-insurance payouts after the deaths and to whom they were paid.

But then she realized there was more at stake than

simply life insurance. The newspaper headline on the microfiche in front of her was dated six months after the murders and the headline on this day was all about a new highway being built. She'd driven in on a highway. She assumed it was the one referenced here, but when she looked closely at the map, it showed a different route—one that appeared to go right through the property that had once belonged to Paul and Rene Renfield.

She printed off that map, then shut down the microfiche and gathered her things. She glanced at her watch. If she hurried, she could get over to the county clerk's office before they closed for lunch. She wanted to find out who now owned the property. Obviously, a highway had never been built there, but if someone had gotten ahold of the plans ahead of time and known about the proposed route, it was the perfect reason to commit murder because they could sell the property for a lot of money.

Lila had Dana's pages already off the printer by the time she got back downstairs. Glancing at the papers, Lila gave her a slight smile.

"Looks like you're on the trail of something," she noted.

Dana couldn't stop the nervous excitement that flowed from her. "I just might be." Had she finally stumbled upon something that explained the need to murder an entire family? She wished she had already gotten herself a new cell phone so she could call Quinn and let him in on her new lead. Truly, she just wanted to talk to him, to hear his voice and enjoy the way his deep baritone warmed her.

She grabbed her stuff and approached Deputy Jenkins. "I need to go to the city clerk's office."

"No problem. I go where you go."

She waved goodbye to Lila and headed to the parking lot. Deputy Jenkins opened her door then closed it after she slipped into the passenger's seat and walked around to the driver's side. As he did, Dana spotted a figure running from the corner of the next building. Reed Jessup! She would know his face anywhere.

Before she could warn Jenkins, Jessup drew a gun and started firing at the car. Dana screamed as Jenkins opened the car door and fell inside, blood pouring from shots to his shoulder and leg. He grabbed his gun and did his best to return fire, but Jessup kept coming.

He grabbed up the radio. "This is Jenkins 324. Shooting at the library. I'm hit. Send backup now. We're under attack."

She couldn't hear the dispatcher's response over the gunfire that Reed Jessup kept firing.

"Run, Dana," Jenkins said, his voice no more than a groan. "Run and hide. Backup is on the way." He lifted his gun again and fired, but she knew he was right. Backup wouldn't arrive in time.

She crawled into the back seat and nearly fell out the back door of the vehicle. Amidst the firing, she ran back into the library. Those inside had heard the shots and were hiding under tables and behind desks.

"Dana, what's happening?" Lila asked, poking her head up from behind the circulation desk.

"It's Reed Jessup. He's got a gun. Stay down. Police are on the way."

She ran through to the stairway and hurried upstairs. Jessup was after her, so hopefully he wouldn't bother targeting Lila or anyone else he saw. She couldn't stop him, but she hated to think others might be harmed because of her.

The downstairs door burst open and Reed fired up the staircase as Dana rushed through the second-floor door.

Great. What did she do now? She had to hide from him until the police arrived to help her. She scanned the room and quickly sized it up. The bathrooms were the first place he would look, or possibly the room with the microfiche. If he found her in, either, she was a sitting duck. She had to stay out in the open without limiting herself.

She hurried into the stacks. If she could keep moving and keep him searching the rows of books for her, she might survive long enough for help to arrive. Her mind immediately went to Quinn. She wished he was coming, but with his leg, he wouldn't be able to do much. Still, she knew he would try. She trusted Jenkins and Rich, and even Sheriff Dawson, but not as much as she trusted Quinn.

She stopped and crouched down, listening to the heavy footfalls and deep breathing of Reed as he moved throughout the stacks. Whenever she saw him or heard him nearby, she quietly slipped to another area of the stacks.

"You can't hide from me forever, Miss Lang," Reed's deep voice warned. "I will find you."

She nearly giggled at the idea that he addressed her so formally, but caught herself. It was just a re-action to fear that made her mind go so crazy. But if it was true that Reed Jessup was only a gun for hire, it was possible he didn't even know her first name.

This was nothing but a job for him, but it was her life. And she wasn't giving up without a fight.

Quinn was on the phone listening to his brother outline everything they'd dug up on Reed Jessup. He opened a text from Rich and saw the face of the man who'd attacked them in the woods pop up on his screen. Dana had been right in her identification. Reed Jessup was definitely their man.

"I haven't seen Reed in years. I didn't even rec-ognize him."

"I'm not surprised. He was several years behind you in school and you haven't been here for his mul-tiple arrests on drug charges."

His brother paused. "By the way, Dana said to tell you she'd be by later. She was asking me how you were."

"I'm fine."

"Be careful, Quinn. She's coming to your house. If you're not going to tell her then be sure to hide anything that might give it away."

His eye went to the photo of him and Tommy

taken near a remote village in Libya. They'd worked four contract jobs together in the past five years, after each leaving their respective Special Forces detail. And it was no secret that Tommy Woods had died during the embassy rescue. Rich was right. Quinn kicked himself for not realizing that Dana would zero in on that photograph.

He hated having to hide this part of his life from her. His time with Delta and with SOA defined him as a soldier and a warrior. He'd given his whole life to fighting for other people, to being away from his home and family for months and years on end. But now he found himself wondering what it would be like to have a reason to return home. To see a lovely, smiling face instead of just his old hound dogs. He'd told himself that seeing Rich with a wife and a family didn't affect him, but he'd been lying. He wanted what his brother had, but he'd never been able to fathom how to make it work with his wandering lifestyle. A wife would want him home with her, not off in another country fighting for peace.

Somehow, his mind was already fitting Dana into that role, only she didn't fit well with his image of a wife and family. He couldn't peg her as a wife who would sit around waiting for her husband to return home. She traveled with her own work, investigating cold cases and exposing men's secrets on television for all the world to see.

He sat on the bed and put his head in his hands. It didn't matter what his image of a wife looked like because he wouldn't be going anywhere once Dana uncovered his secret. Only God knew what his life would look like then, and God wasn't talking to him. No, scratch that. Quinn wasn't listening.

He'd spent the past few weeks since returning home grieving his friend's loss. He'd only met Mike a few days before the attack, but Tommy had been like his brother and Quinn had loved him as much as he loved Rich. He should have been able to save him. Or at the very least, died in his place. He'd left Tommy's side for only a few minutes during the attack, but they'd been the most important minutes of Quinn's life.

No, he had to put the brakes on this thing with Dana. It couldn't end well. He saw no future with her except the one where she plastered his face all over the country as one of the SOA operatives who'd been present during the embassy attack. He couldn't allow any more of his brothers to die like that. He had to be there to protect them when it mattered and he couldn't be there, wouldn't be there, if Dana Lang learned his secret.

His bible was sitting on the nightstand. His mornings had once consisted of grabbing it first thing and spending time in the Word, but not recently. He'd placed it there after returning home, but he hadn't opened it. He didn't want to hear God's explanations about why Tommy died and he had lived. He didn't want to be reminded that it was God's plan. He didn't care whose plan it was. He didn't like it. Tommy had a wife and kids. Quinn had none. It should have been him.

Quinn heard his brother's radio cackle and a commotion in the office over the line. "What's happening?" Quinn asked.

Rich let out a breath. "We just found Reed Jessup. He's at the library."

"Dana," Quinn called out, realizing she would be there. "Where's Jenkins? Is he still with her?"

He heard his brother's voice catch. "He's been shot. I'm on my way there now."

Quinn could hear his brother running outside to his car and sliding into the passenger's seat. When he heard the whir of the siren, he jumped up.

"I'm on my way, too."

"You can't do anything. You can barely walk."

"Dana's there. I'm coming."

He slammed down the phone and grabbed his crutches. He didn't care if he was injured or in pain. He needed to be there. He needed to make sure she was safe.

He grabbed his phone again and dialed her cell. It went to voice mail. He didn't know if that was because she hadn't yet managed to get a new one after the wreck, or because she was physically unable to answer. He prayed it was the first option.

God, please keep her safe.

He made it to his spare car and started the engine. It sputtered and resisted, but finally roared to life. He jammed it into gear and took off, praying that he wasn't heading into a murder scene. He wasn't sure his heart could take another loss.

Dana crouched behind a row of books. She put her head in her hands as tears threatened to overtake her. She couldn't cry now. She had to keep her wits about her if she was going to survive, but she was beginning to become overwhelmed. Who wanted her dead? And why?

She suddenly realized the person who knew was within earshot. It was a dangerous move to out her location to someone chasing her, but she couldn't pass up the opportunity to know.

"Why are you doing this?" she called out to Reed. "What have I ever done to you?"

She heard him move, slowly, sure-footed, as he calculated her position, but he didn't respond to those questions.

She had others. "Who are you working for, Reed? Who wants me dead and why? You should at least tell me who if you're going to kill me."

He chuckled, a dark, crazy kind of laugh, but didn't answer her question directly. "I told you why. You're sticking your nose where it doesn't belong."

"So this is about the Renfield case? Someone doesn't want me finding answers, do they? Why? Did the person who hired you kill Rene and Alicia?"

She heard movement at the end of the row and realized he was getting too close. She couldn't keep talking…but how could she not ask when she had the opportunity?

From outside, the sound of sirens filled the air. She could see flashes of lights as the sheriff's office arrived on the scene. She heard Reed swear then rush to the window to look outside. He must not have liked what he saw because he spun to address her again.

"They won't save you. You'll be dead before anyone can stop me."

She leaned against a stack of books and it gave a little. She realized she had the perfect opportunity to fight back. Pushing at the shelves as hard as she could, she felt them move. A moment later, one shelf hit another then another and that one toppled onto Reed Jessup. She heard him grunt as piles of books rained down on him.

But she didn't stick around to make sure it disabled him. She took off running back through the stairwell door and downstairs, and finally burst through the door at the bottom. She was met by at least ten guns aimed her way.

"Don't shoot," the lead deputy stated and she realized it was Rich. He approached her. "Where's Reed?"

"Upstairs. I pushed the shelves onto him."

He motioned for the others to follow him and they ran past her.

She watched them enter the stairwell, then she headed for the front of the library. She could see the main floor had been cleared out already. Pushing through the doors, she saw Quinn hobbling toward her on crutches. Finally, he dropped them and rushed to her. She ran to him and fell into his arms. Only then did she allow the tears to come freely.

"It's okay, Dana. I've got you. I would have been inside if they would have let me."

She didn't care about that. All she cared about was that this ordeal was over and she was safe in Quinn Dawson's arms. She never wanted to leave them again.

She felt Quinn tense and turned to see Rich and the others exit the library.

Rich shook his head. "He wasn't there."

"He was," Dana insisted. "I knocked the books over on top of him. I heard them pound him. He couldn't have gotten up that quickly."

"He did. He must have found another way out. I've got men searching the building and we'll start a search party for the perimeter. Don't worry, we'll find him."

Quinn squeezed her against him. "Let's get you out of here. I'm taking you to the hospital."

Rich nodded. "Good idea. I'll have Montgomery drive you."

Dana stopped, suddenly remembering the deputy who'd tried to protect her. "What happened to Deputy Jenkins. Is he okay?"

Rich's expression turned grim. "Last I heard, he took three bullets and was unconscious by the time we arrived on scene. He's being taken straight to surgery. They don't know if he'll make it."

Sorrow washed through her. "I want to go see him. He saved my life."

"I'll keep you updated," Rich told his brother before heading for a cruiser and climbing inside. The new deputy Rich had assigned to protect her climbed into the driver's seat, but Dana could tell he would rather be out looking for Reed Jessup than driving them to the hospital.

Jenkins had been one of their own and Dana knew from experience that Reed had painted an even bigger target on himself by shooting the deputy. In a strange way, that gave her some assurance that they definitely wouldn't stop until they found Reed Jessup.

SIX

Quinn pushed back the curtain as the doctor finished stitching a nasty cut on Dana's arm. She hadn't even realized she'd cut it until Quinn pointed it out. It must have happened when she'd fallen out of the car while running from Jessup. She sat up on the hospital bed. She was beat up and weary from her ordeal with her assailant and wanted nothing more than to find him and end this once and for all.

But she couldn't relax knowing a good man like Deputy Jenkins was fighting for his life for protecting her. "How is Jenkins?"

She knew it would be bad news before he even said it. "He's still in surgery. Things aren't looking good."

Anger rushed through her and she wanted to cry. Quinn took her hand. "It wasn't your fault. You don't need to focus on that right now."

The doctor finished her arm. "This might be sore, but you're fortunate it wasn't worse. I'll go get your release papers."

He exited the room, leaving Quinn and Dana alone. Suddenly, the urge to cry intensified and as tears fell, Quinn pulled her into his embrace.

"I don't know what happened," she stated. "He appeared out of nowhere when we were getting into the car. I thought I would follow up on a lead that might reveal the killer's motives, but Reed was there. I even tried to get him to tell me who wanted me dead, but he kept that information close to his chest."

He used his thumb to wipe a tear from her cheek. "I'm sorry this keeps happening. We'll figure it out."

He was right. She couldn't spend all her time focusing on Deputy Jenkins, or even on Reed Jessup. She had to press on. "What about your grandfather's notes? Do you feel up to going to get them now? They might shed some light on who's behind this."

He nodded. "Sure. That's a good idea. I'll call my dad and let him know we're heading to my place. I'm sure he'll want to ask you some questions later."

Once she received her discharge papers, they walked outside to his car and headed to his house. She was aware that the last time they'd made this journey, they'd been attacked and knew he was on the lookout for Reed or someone else coming after them. She grimaced as they passed the area where they'd been run off the road, but this time, no cars tried to kill them.

They arrived at the house and Quinn led her to the shop in the back. He used a key to undo the padlock, then pushed open the door, revealing a ton of furniture and boxes, all piled on top of other furniture.

"I've kept this locked up since my grandfather's death, but I helped pack every box of his belongings. If he'd kept files about the case—and I recall seeing him with them—they have to be inside that secret compartment I noticed as a child."

He pushed boxes aside until he'd made a trail to the back of the shed, then he grabbed a stepladder. When he discarded the crutches, intent on starting up the ladder, she stopped him. "You shouldn't be doing that with your bad ankle. Let me."

She stepped onto the ladder and pushed at the door in the ceiling until it gave. Inside, she spotted a box containing an accordion folder, a binder and a leather-bound journal.

"I think this is it," she told him, excitement bubbling up in her voice.

This find might hold all the answers she'd been searching for and it had been hidden in this attic for years.

She pulled out a binder and opened it. "It looks like laboratory reports." She glanced at one of the pages and excitement burst through her. "It has Rene's name on it."

"Hand it down to me."

She passed him the binder then reached for the accordion file and journal. However, as she went to hand them to him, she lost her balance and fell, tumbling backward.

He dropped the binder and caught her, his strong arms wrapping protectively around her as he lowered her to the floor. She glanced up at him. They'd never been this close before and she suddenly couldn't concentrate on even putting words together to form a sentence. She quivered as he ran his hands up her arms and she felt a rush of excitement fill her. Never before had being this close to someone felt so right.

He pushed a strand of hair from her face, his knuckles grazing her cheek. She shuddered at the sudden sensation that rushed through her. She looked at him now, his green eyes warm and bright. She was comfortable with him and he made her feel at home. Somehow, he and this town had wrestled their way under her skin and become important to her. He was someone she trusted, and she didn't trust easily. She realized that for the first time in a long while she hadn't given Jason a second thought. And what had seemed like such an intense connection with her ex-boyfriend was nothing compared to the growing feelings she had for Quinn Dawson.

He didn't move his hand from her face. Instead, he stroked her cheek, then her lips with his finger. He leaned in close and she knew he was about to kiss her. More than that, she wanted him to.

But this wasn't the time or place to be delving into her personal feelings for Quinn. A murderer was on the loose, and she was no closer to proving she was Alicia Renfield than she had been before she came to town.

She stepped away from him and his arms fell to his sides. "Thank you for catching me," she said, her voice hoarse with emotion. She cleared it. "I guess we should get this stuff inside so we can go through it."

He seemed to understand, not taking offense at her hesitation. He gave her a long, hard stare then nodded and picked up his crutches. She kneeled and returned the contents that had spilled when she'd fallen. She carried them outside, always aware of his eyes on her, watching her every move and knowing that she'd wanted that kiss as much as he had.

As they headed toward the house, she remembered how she'd felt leaving him alone in that truck and when she'd heard the gunshots. She'd been devastated at the thought that he might be dead and ecstatic when she'd seen him in the woods. Why was she fighting her attraction to Quinn? For the first time in a long time, she was spending time with someone who made her feel appreciated.

They headed into his house and started rummaging through the files. Most of what she saw looked to be standard evidence and not the smoking gun she'd been hoping to find.

"These are all lab and autopsy reports for Rene," he told her. "Looks like pretty routine stuff except for one thing."

"What's that?"

"There's only reports about Rene. Nothing in here for Alicia. If she really died that night, where are her lab and autopsy reports?"

He shot her a knowing look and she shuddered. One more indicator that she was right.

The accordion folder contained evidence documentation and forensic information, as well as photographs of the scene. She pulled out one photo and stared at it, gasping at the image of what was left of the deceased woman. She was no stranger to crime-scene photos, but knowing that this victim might be her mother made it different, much more personal. A tear slipped from her eye and she wiped it away. Quinn must have noticed because he gently caressed her arm. "You don't have to do this," he told her.

She had to maintain her composure if she was going to get through this. She had to be detached, because if she examined this evidence like the daughter of a murder victim, she would never uncover the truth. She had to do her best to hold on to her professional demeanor. "Yes, I do," she said, then continued digging into the information in the folder.

Quinn picked up the journal and flipped through it. "These are my grandfather's personal notes on the case over the years." He stopped and read several pages. "It looks like he never believed Paul was the killer."

He handed her the journal. This was what she'd been searching for. Was the reason Bill Mackey had left her at the church mentioned in the pages of this journal? She flipped through pages and pages of handwritten notes, personal thoughts, questions he had about the case and revelations of the man she was sure was behind this entire cover-up. And every page was filled. A rush of excitement overcame her.

"It's a lot of information," she said.

He nodded. "I told you this case troubled him. He spent years going over it piece by piece. He never forgot about it. My guess is you'll find entries in there from a few weeks after the murders until almost the day he died."

He apparently wrote extensively about the murder and included his own thoughts, but had he written anything about her, about abandoning a child or his reasons for doing so? And why had he never told anyone, not even his family, about that long-held secret? "Why do you think he never told anyone about me?"

"I don't know. I suppose because he never found the real killer."

"I've been thinking about why he did what he did—leaving me at that church." She'd been trying to work through the anger she felt over being abandoned, but it was hard to get past no matter what his intentions had been. "He must have believed I was in real danger from someone."

"I think so, too."

"Tell me about him, Quinn. I can see he was dedicated to this case from this information, but what kind of man was he personally?"

"He was a great man. He taught me everything I know about life and honor and integrity. He was the first one who made me really want to help fight injustice in the world. He's the reason I joined the army instead of the sheriff's office."

"How did your family feel about that?"

"Oh, they worried about me, especially when I joined Delta."

"You were a Delta operator?" She wasn't at all surprised to learn that he'd held a Special Forces job, but she was surprised he was sharing this information with her. "They're a very elite group of warriors."

"I worked hard to earn that distinction and I was good at it. Being a soldier is all I've ever known."

"I guess private security isn't quite as thrilling, is it?"

"It has its moments, but it's nice to be able to use my skills. One thing I learned during my time in the army was that this world is so much bigger than this little town. Don't get me wrong, I love it here. This is home. But it's not everything. There's a big world out there and there's a lot of evil to be fought."

She understood what he was saying. She saw evil in her job every day. And being surrounded by it all the time could have an effect on your soul. It was good he could come home to a place like West Bend to relax and refresh. She'd never really had such a place and she found herself jealous. She wasn't comparing her job reporting on cold cases to what he'd done in Delta, or even the physical dangers he faced now on his job in private security, but she understood how seeing such violence could affect a person.

She was glad to hear more about Bill Mackey from someone who knew him best. He sounded like a good man and everything she'd read in the archives had him pinned as a decent sheriff. By all accounts, if he'd left her with that preacher then he'd likely had a good reason for doing so. It must have been for her protection. She wanted to believe that. She wanted to believe Quinn's grandfather was good and had her best interests at heart.

But she couldn't seem to throw off the anger that still came whenever she thought about it. He'd left her there, alone and helpless. She put her face in her hands, wanting to cry. She'd been excited about the possibility of being that abandoned little girl, but now she was terrified at what it might reveal—that the real reason Bill Mackey had left her at that church was that she wasn't good enough to keep. It was the secret fear that had driven her most of her life. She hadn't been good enough for her adoptive mother to want to spend time with her, for Jason to want to marry her, or for a good and honorable man to take the time to find her a decent home.

"Hey, it's going to be okay," Quinn said, seeing her emotional struggle.

He pulled her into an embrace and she laid her head against his chest and leaned back, never wanting this moment to end. She was finally in a good place, finally able to move on from the hurt and pain Jason had caused her. But how could she fall for Quinn when she didn't even know who she was or where she belonged?

A sound behind Dana caused them both to turn to see Quinn's parents walking inside. "We don't mean to interrupt," Clara said. "John told me what happened and I wanted to make sure you were all okay."

"Thank you for your concerns," Dana told her. "I'm more worried about Deputy Jenkins's condition. Have you heard anything?"

"Jenkins is still in surgery but they're listing his status as critical," Sheriff Dawson told her.

"What about Reed Jessup?"

"He's still on the loose, but we're scouring the area. We will find him." He turned to Quinn and the papers they'd been sorting through. "Have you found anything?"

"It looks like Grandpa took the evidence from the file," Quinn told his father. He'd found scores of notes so far on inconsistencies in the records and evidence logs.

"Why would he do that knowing it would make prosecuting anyone for the crimes impossible?"

"According to his notes, he believed someone in the office was already compromising the evidence. He didn't know who it was, but he was convinced someone was working against the sheriff's office. He must have believed it would never be prosecuted. Which means he knew Rene's killer would always be free. Alicia would always be in danger if her attempted killer couldn't be prosecuted."

He glanced at Dana. It made sense, more sense than anything else about this situation. His grandfather would have wanted to do what was best for her.

She seemed to understand that. "So he faked my death in order to keep me safe from a killer who was apparently unstoppable?"

It sounded like his grandfather, except for one additional thing. "But he never gave up looking. He went to his grave trying to keep you safe."

"That sounds like Dad," Clara stated. She put an arm around Dana's shoulders and hugged her tightly.

Quinn noticed a tear slip from her eye at his mother's embrace and she suddenly seemed flustered. "Thank you. I only found out about all this recently and I have to admit I've been dealing with some anger over why he would just abandon me that way. Now, I see he was only trying to protect me."

"I can't imagine what he was going through. He must not have known who to trust."

John grimaced. "I wish he would have trusted me. I was young and new back then but he had a lot of years to confide in me. Maybe I could have helped clear this case before now."

Clara gave him a knowing look. "He didn't want to burden you with what he'd done."

"Well, there was too much nonburdening back then and not enough following the law." He grumbled then pulled several sheets of paper from his pocket. "We found some papers around Jenkins's cruiser. I assume they were yours?"

Quinn glanced over her shoulder and saw they were copies of an aerial map.

Dana nodded. "Yes, they are. I saw this in the newspaper archives and I was heading to the clerk's office to check it out. Apparently, there was a proposal for a new highway and the Renfield property ran through it."

"I remember that," Clara stated and her husband nodded.

"Paul refused to sell. That land had been in his family for generations."

"What happened to it after he died?"

"With no heirs, it was eventually auctioned off and purchased by a developer, I think. But the highway plans changed. It ended up not going anywhere near the Renfield property."

His heart kicked up a notch at this new development. "Would that have been a reason to kill an entire family?" Quinn asked. He'd seen greed in his life, but it still shocked him when it hit this close to home."

"It's worth considering," his father stated. "Why don't you two follow up with the clerk's office and find out who purchased that property and when. I'll look in to when the highway plans were changed."

Quinn nodded, but Dana spoke up.

"I had some questions about Paul and Rene and I was hoping, since you've both mentioned knowing them, that you could answer some things for me. I heard the rumors that Rene was thinking of leaving Paul for someone else. Is there any truth to those rumors?"

Quinn saw them glance at one another then hesitate. He knew that shared look. They were about to shut down her questioning.

Before they could, Dana said, "I know they were your friends and you don't want to do anything to damage their memories, but someone is trying to kill me for looking into this. I need to know the truth. Was Rene planning to leave Paul for another man?"

His mom fidgeted but told what she knew. "I can't say for certain that she was going to leave Paul, but she'd had an affair with her old boyfriend a while back. In fact, most people thought Alicia was his child and not Paul's. What she told me was that he wanted to get back together with her, but she was conflicted about what to do."

Quinn could see Dana was rocked by this new information. It was one thing to learn your father had murdered your mother and tried to kill you, but now to learn that your father may not have been your real father. It was mind-blowing.

His dad agreed. "Paul was concerned that she was going to leave him, but he was prepared to fight for her. He didn't want to lose his family."

"Who was this old boyfriend?" Dana asked. "Has anyone looked into him?" She turned back to the records they'd been searching through and looked at Quinn. "Did you see anything about this old boyfriend?"

"It was Calvin Jessup."

Dana looked shocked when his mother said the man's name. He was shocked, too. "Mayor Jessup? Rene was having an affair with Mayor Jessup?"

"Well, he wasn't mayor then. Calvin and Rene were high-school sweethearts. He broke it off when he went away to college and law school, but he and Rene always had a thing for one another. When he returned home, Rene was already married to Paul and Calvin was set to marry Meredith. Still, he told her he wanted to be with her. I heard he even broke off his engagement to Meredith so Rene would see he was serious about being with her."

Quinn turned to his father. "I know he was your friend, but what makes you believe Paul wasn't the killer?"

"In my job, I've seen people do terrible things to one another. I would never cross Paul out as a suspect because he's my friend. The facts are that he's never been found. There's never even been a sighting of him in all these years. His social security number and bank accounts have never been touched since the night of the fire. My professional opinion is that Paul died that night along with his family but his body has never been discovered. I believe whoever committed those horrible acts hid his body to make him a scapegoat and divert attention from the actual killer. I watched my father-in-law go over that evidence night after night while I was still on the force. I saw those evidence reports before they vanished from the official file. Paul's blood was found at the scene. It was a significant amount. Something terrible happened to him that night and as far as we know, he never received any medical attention. I believe that's why Bill never bought in to the Paul-as-the-killer scenario."

"But why would Calvin kill the woman he loved and his own child?"

"Maybe she refused to leave Paul?" his mom suggested.

But Quinn had a more obvious answer. "Or because an illegitimate child could ruin a politician's career path."

He looked to his father. They needed to have a candid conversation with Mayor Jessup, but Quinn knew the man wielded a lot of power in town. He'd held the position of mayor for nearly twenty years and had made several failed bids for governor before setting his sights on a senate seat in Washington. Having a presumed dead illegitimate daughter suddenly appear could derail yet another bid for political office.

His father sighed. "It's not enough to compel him to talk to us, but maybe I can convince him to come in to answer a few questions. He has to know that if we're investigating this case he'll be called in to answer questions. I'll go back to the department and make the call."

"Drop me home first?" Clara asked and he nodded. "We'll see you both later," she said, then walked out with her husband.

Dana turned back to the papers from his grandfather's stack, but she seemed lost now. He had to admit his own mind was whirling with all the new information they'd just learned.

He realized for the first time that they were kindred spirits. They both hated injustice in the world and tried to do away with it, her through her exposés and him through his military service and security work.

Why was he fighting her? They both wanted the same thing—to find the truth and bring it to light.

He pulled her to him and held her close. The smell of her soap floated over his skin, captivating him, drawing him like a moth to a flame. But would he get burned by her? She lifted her head and looked up at him, her eyelashes wet with tears. She seemed so vulnerable now that it drew out in him the desire to protect her, but he knew better than anyone that this lady in his arms didn't need protection. She could take care of herself. She'd proven that to him. But he couldn't squelch the urge to pull her from danger and do whatever it took to keep her safe from the world.

Her hand grazed his arm, sending chills through him. He breathed a deep breath and suddenly found it difficult to swallow with her so close. He could claim her lips with only a tilt of his head and the way they parted seemed to welcome him to do so.

His hand tightened on her back and he pulled her even closer. She closed her eyes and lifted her face to his, their lips only inches apart.

But did he really want to go down this road with her? Was he ready for this level of commitment? He wouldn't lead her on. Either he wanted a relationship with her or he didn't, but he couldn't, could he? He would never be able to trust that she would keep his secret. It wasn't right to burden her with such a secret and never allow her to tell it. It wouldn't be fair to her.

She took the initiative before he did, closing the inches between them, and suddenly the soft, suppleness of her mouth muddled his thinking. He pulled her close against him and it felt right, like a missing part of him had suddenly been found. He wanted to keep it with him and never let it go again, sparking a fire deep in his soul, alerting him to something that had been missing in his life that he hadn't even realized.

They stayed that way for a long time, wrapped in each other's arms, her head on his chest, his hand stroking her hair. And it felt right. It felt good.

Quinn hadn't had many dealings with Mayor Jessup, but he knew from watching the news that the mayor liked to make a statement wherever he went. Today was no exception. The mayor arrived at the sheriff's office in two large, black SUVs with tinted windows and a procession led by a local West Bend officer. He was impeccably dressed in a suit and tie and offered a big smile and brisk hand shake when Quinn's father greeted him.

"I appreciate you coming by, Calvin," John Dawson told him.

"Of course," Jessup assured him. "Meredith and I are both very upset about this mess with Reed. We'll do whatever we can to help, but frankly, I haven't heard from him in weeks. I usually don't when he's strung out."

John Dawson stopped in front of Quinn. "You remember my younger son, Quinn?"

"Of course, the Delta guy. That was a nasty business in Libya a few weeks back, wasn't it?"

Quinn tried not to show it but he flinched at the mayor's words. He didn't make his business known around town, but rumors were hard to stop and many people knew he'd been out of the country at the same time as the embassy attack. He also knew his family had requested special prayers during the hours they had no idea if he was dead or alive. Small-town rumors were hard to stifle. And Dana was close by, listening to the exchange from an interview room, where she was hiding until Jessup was ushered through the department. Given that several people had commented on how much she looked like Rene, it had been her idea to remain out of sight until the right moment to spring on Calvin Jessup and demand to know the truth about what had happened that night. Now…had she heard the mayor's comment about Libya? And how long did he really think he could continue hiding it from her?

"Yes, it was, Mayor. Almost as nasty as this business with your nephew."

He nodded and grew solemn. "Yes, Reed is a troubled boy."

"He's not a boy anymore. He's twenty-three and he shot a cop."

Quinn watched as a political mask seemed to drop from the mayor's face. He imagined for the first time he was seeing the man instead of the politician. "What do you mean he shot a cop? No one's told me that. My chief only said there was an incident involving Reed at the library." He turned to Quinn's father. "What's happened?"

John Dawson led him into an interview room. "Let's talk in here."

He went inside and closed the door. Quinn walked to the secondary interview room, where Dana was waiting. They were able to both see and hear what was going on inside the other room.

"John? Tell me the truth? Reed shot someone?"

"He did. He ambushed Deputy Mike Jenkins today at the public library and shot him three times. The doctors are still uncertain if he's going to make it."

"But why? Why would he do that?"

"Jenkins was assigned to a protection detail. It seems Reed has been trying to attack a woman in town for the past few days. Dana Lang. Have you heard of her?"

"The news lady? I know her name and I'd heard she was in town, but why would Reed want to harm her?"

She nudged closer to Quinn when Jessup started talking about her and he wrapped his arm around her, not even caring at this point what anyone thought. She needed his support and he was going to give it without reservation.

"That's what we're trying to find out," John insisted. "Have a seat."

"I should phone Meredith and let her know. I had no idea Reed was involved in the shootout at the library. I'm sorry, John."

"Before you call her, I'd like to ask you some questions. Please, take a seat."

Quinn noticed that the attitude in the room seemed to shift as the mayor realized this wasn't just an informational meeting about Reed. "What's this about?"

His father stood again, his size intimidating as he faced Calvin Jessup, and for the first time Quinn realized what a formidable man his father was. "Reed attacked Miss Lang and my son Quinn yesterday and tried to kill them. They both identified him as the attacker. And now, today, Miss Lang is certain it was the same man. We also have multiple witnesses at the library when he started shooting that corroborate her account. The thing is, we have evidence that he may not be acting alone. We believe his attacks on Miss Lang have been orchestrated by someone else."

"That makes sense. I can't imagine what he would have against a woman he doesn't even know. Someone must be paying him. He's a heroin addict. He would do just about anything for money to buy more drugs."

John nodded. "You say you haven't spoken to Reed in weeks?"

"Am I being accused of something, John?"

"No. Right now, we're still in the asking-questions phase of our investigation."

"Aside from Reed being my nephew, what possible reason would I have to want to harm a TV reporter?"

"Because she's in town looking into the old Renfield murder."

Jessup stood and folded his arms as the realization of why he was really called here seemed to hit home. "Ah. I see. And I'm once again the prime suspect? Is that right?"

"The fact of the matter is, Calvin, that you've never actually been cleared as a suspect in Rene's murder."

"I didn't want her dead, John. I loved her. I would never have killed her."

Dana glanced up at Quinn. His father had told her to come in at Jessup's mention of loving Rene. "That's my cue." She walked from the room and he caught sight of her again as she opened the door and stepped into the interview room.

Jessup turned to look at her. His eyes widened in shock and he took several steps backward as he watched her.

"Mayor Calvin Jessup, this is Miss Dana Lang."

"I'm sorry," Jessup said of his reaction. "It's just that you look very much like someone I used to know."

"Rene Renfield?"

He nodded almost involuntarily. Finally, he managed to croak out a yes.

But Dana was unaffected by his loss of composure. She was cool and calm as she approached him, her eyes refusing to give away any detail of the raging emotion she must be feeling as she confronted this man who might be her father, and her mother's killer.

"That's because I'm her daughter."

Mayor Jessup looked as freaked out as Dana felt at the moment.

"No, that's not possible. Alicia was her only child and she died in the fire."

His shock seemed genuine, but then again, if he was the killer, he'd spent years believing he'd gotten away with a double—or triple—murder. "That's what everyone believes, but it's not true. Alicia didn't die that night. Instead, she—I—was left at a church several days after the fire. My identity was hidden and I was adopted, but I'm Alicia Renfield."

"Alicia? Alive?" He looked at John for confirmation. "Is this true?"

Sheriff Dawson came to her aid. "Her story seems to add up. And given the fact that someone has been trying to kill her since she came to town, I tend to believe it."

"But how did this happen? Why does everyone believe she died all those years ago?"

"I believe my grandfather was worried about her safety," Quinn stated from behind her, entering the room. She sighed. She hadn't known he was coming in, too, but she felt better having him so close.

"He worried that whoever killed Rene wanted Alicia dead, too."

"But Paul—"

"We've never been able to name Paul as the killer," Sheriff Dawson stated. "In fact, I personally believe he died that night along with his wife."

Jessup scrubbed a hand over his face and paced the small room. He stared at the table as the shock of the situation changed to realization. "You all think I was behind this. You think I killed them all. Why? Because she rejected me?"

"Did she reject you?" Dana asked. She wanted to learn everything this man knew about that terrible night's events.

He looked at her and nodded. "She did. She wanted to try to make her marriage work. Also, she wasn't interested in being a politician's wife and I had my sights set on a career in politics. But I would never have killed her over something like that. I'll admit I was heartbroken, but why would I kill them?"

Quinn gave his mother's answer. "Because an illegitimate child with a married girlfriend might be enough to halt a political career before it even got started."

Dana stepped forward. "And an illegitimate daughter of a murdered woman could end one in its path."

He stared at her, but shook his head. "If this is true, Miss Lang, if you truly are Rene's and my daughter, I can guarantee you I would be nothing but thrilled. If my political aspirations are that shallow, then perhaps I shouldn't be in politics to begin with."

"Are you claiming, Mayor, that you aren't behind your nephew's attacks?"

"I am not. As I've stated, I haven't been in touch with Reed in weeks. I certainly haven't paid him to attack anyone. If I were looking for ways to end my political career, that would certainly do it." He stared at her and there was a sort of admiration in his eyes. Was he really seeing her mother in her face? "You know, I've seen you on television before but I never noticed how much you look like Rene. It's not only the looks. You move like her. You even sound like her."

She wasn't sure how to respond to this. Was this man her true father?

But suddenly his demeanor changed again and the politician's face she'd noticed earlier went up. "Looks aside, may I ask what evidence you have that makes you believe you're Rene's daughter? After all, there was a funeral. Are you claiming they buried an empty coffin?"

"We don't have those answers yet," Sheriff Dawson admitted.

"Well, I think the next logical step would be to exhume the grave and make certain there's no body inside that coffin. I can arrange to have a judge sign the order of exhumation."

She glanced at Quinn who looked at his father. Sheriff Dawson agreed. "We've already contacted the county attorney to set up a meeting with the judge for that."

"Well, maybe I can get that hearing date sped up." Jessup stopped to gaze at Dana. He looked like he wanted to reach out to her to stroke her face and make certain she was real, but he stopped himself before making contact. "If this is true, if you do turn out to be my daughter, I hope we'll get to have another conversation. Hopefully not in a police interrogation room next time, though."

He walked out. Dana watched him leave the sheriff's office and climb back into his SUV. He was already on the phone, probably calling his wife to let her know about the situation with their nephew. She was conflicted about meeting him. Was this the man who'd given her life? Or the man who'd tried to take her life as a child? Or both?

SEVEN

By that evening, Dana was back at the hotel packing her bags. Quinn had insisted she come stay at his home and, honestly, she was glad for the offer. The memory of being trapped by Reed Jessup and not knowing if she would live or die made her shudder. She'd come so close to dying that it frightened her.

Quinn came up behind her. He must have sensed how being in this room affected her because he wrapped her in his arms and held her close. "We're going to figure this out," he whispered. "It's all going to be okay."

She was thankful for his presence here today, but she was beginning to wonder if they would ever find Reed Jessup before he killed her and if she would ever discover who was behind these attempts on her life. Her confrontation with Mayor Jessup hadn't gotten her any closer to answers. In fact, now she was even more confused. She'd met politicians before and knew they could be two-faced and charming all at once, but she'd believed him, sincerely believed him, when he'd told her he'd loved Rene and could never hurt her.

But someone had harmed her. If not Jessup, then who?

He put his arm around her and pulled her close. "We'll figure this out," he assured her. "We won't stop until we do."

She breathed in the scent of him, leaning into his chest for support. It felt good to have someone on her side for once. She realized how alone she'd felt since her mom died. It felt good to have someone to lean on.

Tracy would say she was falling for Quinn and as much as she wanted to deny it, she couldn't. She looked forward to seeing him each day and he was the first person she thought of each morning. She'd learned to rely on him, to depend on him, and it had been so long since she'd depended on anyone.

She trusted him, and that was as close as she was ready to admit to falling in love. But she couldn't tell him. She wouldn't. Because no matter how good it felt to be in his arms, she knew any relationship she entered was destined to fail. She was born to be alone forever.

She waited until she was settled into Quinn's spare bedroom before she pulled out her new cell phone and called Tracy. She needed to hear her friend's voice and restore some semblance of normalcy to her life. Tracy and her producer and the show were real life. All this—West Bend, Quinn and multiple attempts on her life—was surreal.

"How's it going there?" Tracy asked her.

She touched her neck, remembering the feel of the blade against her skin. "It's been a tough few days. How is everything there?"

"Oh, you know, Mason's freaking out about getting the show together. Basically, normal stuff. How are things going with Mr. Tall, Dark and Handsome?"

"Everything is good." She still hadn't told Tracy the real reason she'd come to West Bend and, quite frankly, she wasn't in the mood to get into it tonight.

"Have you worked out what you wanted to find yet?"

"No, not yet. I need you to do something for me, Tracy. I'm trying to find a man named Jay Englin. He used to be a fireman in West Bend, Missouri."

"Okay, sure. I'll see if I can track him down. Can I tell him what you want with him?"

"I have some questions about something that happened in this town thirty years ago. He'll know what that was if it's truly him. Hey, and can you also check on some insurance payouts for me?" She gave Tracy what she knew about the insurance company and the fire at the Renfield estate.

"Sounds like you're on the track of something," Tracy said excitedly. "Sure you don't need help?"

"Not with this, but if you could keep Mason off my back, that would be great. I know it's a lot to ask."

"You don't know the half of it, Dana. We've been receiving calls at the station about you digging into cases that are better left alone."

That comment made Dana perk up. "Who called?"

"Mason said he'd received calls from several

prominent senatorial offices complaining about you. You must have made someone very powerful angry."

The only person she knew who would have that kind of clout was Calvin Jessup, whose election for senator was upcoming. She sighed. Back to the non-trusting side again.

"What did Mason tell them?"

"Oh, he was eating it up. He thinks you're on the trail of a hot new story that's going to ruffle a lot of feathers. He's super excited about it. Is he right?"

"In a manner of speaking. Feathers are already being ruffled."

"That's obvious. Be careful, Dana."

"I will. Thanks, Tracy. You're the best. I promise I'll explain all this someday soon."

"I imagine it'll be quite a story. I'll keep you updated if I find anything."

She hung up with Tracy and thought about what Mason had told her. If Calvin Jessup was powerful enough to get other senators involved in smearing her name, then he must be used to getting his way around this town as well. She had to place him firmly back into the suspect category.

Maybe he had loved Rene, but people in love often did things they later regretted. Only one person she knew of was left alive who knew the truth and he was doing his best to stay hidden.

Jay Englin, where are you?

Dana would never have imagined things could proceed so quickly, but within two days, she had a date to see the judge and request the exhumation of Rene and Alicia's graves. Once they knew for certain Alicia was not in the coffin, Rene's DNA could be checked against Dana's to confirm she was who she claimed to be. Dana chewed nervously on her fingernail as she sat at the table across from the county prosecutor and waited for her opportunity to present her evidence.

Quinn, sitting behind her, gently took her hand. "Calm down," he said as she fidgeted. "Why are you nervous?"

Why was she? Opening the grave and discovering whether or not Alicia was inside it was the only way to know for sure if Dana was right that the little girl hadn't died that night thirty years ago. Now, one man, Judge Michael Henry, stood between her and her answers.

She glanced around the full courtroom. Somehow, the entire town had heard about her petition to have the grave opened. It appeared most everyone in West Bend was now sitting in the courtroom. She recognized many of them. Customers and staff at the restaurants she'd dined at. Lila and the library staff. Milo, the night clerk at the hotel. Even Mayor Jessup and his wife, Meredith, were present for these proceedings. They'd taken seats behind Dana, and she imagined she could feel daggers in her back from Meredith Jessup, who'd hardly spoken three words to her when they were introduced. Of course, Dana was accusing her nephew of attempted murder and trying to have him thrown in jail while also claiming to be her husband's illegitimate daughter back from the dead, so she supposed that was reason enough for the animosity she felt from Meredith Jessup. The woman obviously wasn't as skilled at hiding her feelings as her politician husband was. The rest of the people present had seen her around town or knew her from her show, she concluded. Perhaps they hoped to be on television. If that was why they'd come, they would be disappointed.

"It's going to be fine," Quinn said. "Stand up and tell the truth. That's what everyone wants to hear."

Dana felt her nerves on edge as the judge entered the courtroom and everyone grew quiet. Colette Williams, the county prosecutor, stood and addressed him.

"Your Honor, we're here today to petition the court to exhume the body of murder victims Rene Renfield and Alicia Renfield. We have new evidence that might refute the official records on the case."

Judge Henry glanced at her. "What exactly is the evidence, Mrs. Williams?"

"We believe Alicia Renfield was not murdered thirty years ago." She glanced at Dana, then continued. "In fact, we have evidence that she's not buried in that grave at all."

An uproar arose in the courtroom and the judge banged his gavel. "Quiet," he demanded and the room hushed after several moments. He turned to Mrs. Williams. "Present your evidence."

She took the papers from Dana and handed them over to the judge. "As you'll see, there's a letter from a preacher whose church was used as a safe haven thirty years ago. In it, he stated someone from this town, someone he trusted, left a baby girl with him believing the child to be in danger. He also claimed the child's parents had both been killed and she was now an orphan. We have a photograph of Alicia Renfield that was used in the media at the time she supposedly perished along with a photograph of the child that was adopted. They're similar enough to give us concern that this child and Alicia Renfield are the same person. We believe that, for whatever reason, someone pretended the child died and buried an empty coffin, but she was actually abandoned several towns over. We would like to have the grave opened to confirm the remains are inside."

Judge Henry glanced at Dana. "I understand you were the one to provide the information, Miss Lang?"

"Yes, Judge." Dana stood, her hands trembling. Although she couldn't see them, she felt all eyes on her. This town of West Bend had come here today to listen as she opened up to the judge about her journey to discover her identity. "I was the one who brought the information to Mrs. Williams. I connected the two cases."

"And what's your interest in this case? I need more of a reason to disturb a child's grave than it's for a television show."

She gulped. This was it. This was the moment the entire world would know her secret once and for all. "This isn't for a show, Judge. This is personal for me. I found those items among my adopted mother's belongings when she died. The little girl that was abandoned was me. I believe I'm Alicia Renfield."

She heard a gasp roar through the crowd and turned. Something popped and whizzed past her. Someone was shooting at her! She screamed and fell, crawling beneath the table as several other shots cracked through the windows of the courtroom. Behind her, Mayor Jessup cried out, then grabbed his shoulder and fell.

His wife clutched her husband and yelled, "He's been shot! Someone's shooting!"

Dana glanced at the mayor, saw the color drain from his face and pain riddle his complexion as people began running screaming from the courtroom.

Bum ankle or not, Quinn leaped over the court gate, his gun drawn and ready. He ran to Dana.

"Are you okay?"

She nodded, her eyes conveying the fear she felt. "I'm not hit," she told him, knowing that was his greatest concern.

He ran to the window, peering out cautiously when it seemed the gunfire had stopped. He didn't want to make himself a target, but he needed to get a look at what was happening. He scanned the tree lines and the buildings, but saw no one who could be the shooter. Likely, he was gone already. Through the window, he spotted people pouring out the doors of the courthouse, doing their best to get free of the building, which seemed incredibly reckless to him because they were heading right into the shooter's line of sight. But as he glanced back at Dana, he knew she had been the only target in this room.

The judge was gone, having been escorted out by the constables during the commotion, and the courtroom had nearly cleared of people. Quinn spotted several deputies and local police officers outside the door doing their best to keep those remaining in the building calm and orderly with little success. He turned to look at the mayor. Pete McKinnon, a local EMT who'd been in the courtroom, had already hurried over and started working on him while Meredith Jessup stood, blood covering her white pantsuit as she held her husband's hand and fussed at Pete to hurry.

"How is he?" Quinn asked Pete.

"Looks like a GSW to the right shoulder. I don't see any more wounds, but this one is bleeding badly. He needs to get to the hospital."

"I'm fine," Mayor Jessup stated, but even his insistence sounded weak. He was breathing heavily and sweating with pain. "I'm sure someone else needs help worse than me."

Meredith Jessup reprimanded him harshly, her fear flowing over into her words. "Hush, Calvin. You've been shot. You need to get to the hospital. You're too important to let something happen to you."

Quinn looked around. No one else seemed to be hit. "It looks like you were the only victim," he stated. He pulled out his cell phone and called for an ambulance, only to discover that one was already on its way because someone else had called in the shots fired.

Quinn had counted four shots. If only one had hit the mayor, what had happened to the remaining three? He scanned the room, quickly finding a trio of bullet holes on the far wall with the bullets still lodged inside. Good, recovering the shells would make identifying the weapon used easier. But Quinn doubted that was going to be necessary.

"What is it?" Dana asked, coming up behind him. "What's wrong?"

He pointed out the trio of bullet holes. "Look how close together they are. That's not random. Whoever fired these shots knew what he was doing."

She glanced back at where the mayor was sitting and where she had been at the time of the shots. "It's not even a direct line from where the mayor was. So these were fired but weren't meant to hit anyone, only scare them."

"Or clear the room," Quinn stated. "More than that, whoever made these shots was an expert marksman."

She turned to look at Mayor Jessup, who was now being loaded onto a gurney by the EMTs. "So he was the target. I thought it was me. But why shoot the mayor?"

Quinn wasn't convinced Jessup had been the target. The angle where he had been sitting was in the direct line of sight from Dana, although it seemed someone trained well enough to make these shots wouldn't have missed and hit the mayor, but even snipers were human and targets often made a little move that changed the situation. Again, he was struck with the blinding anger of realizing she could have been killed today.

Quinn met up with his father and found the sniper's nest where they believed the shots had been made from. He shared his concerns about the shooter being a marksman. "No way Reed Jessup made those shots," he said. "We're looking for someone with either military or law-enforcement training. Someone with sniper experience."

"Who do we know in town that could have made those shots?" his dad asked.

"There aren't many," Rich conceded. "Tim Langley works SWAT with the West Bend police force as a sniper. He's had special training through the state academy. Bruce Davis had sniper training in the US Marines Corps. There are maybe a handful of others in neighboring towns."

John Dawson sighed. "Bruce Davis lost his job at the denim factory six months ago. His wife works at the school with your mother. According to her, they're deep in debt and about to lose their house."

"Any reason he would blame the mayor for that?" Quinn asked.

Rich shrugged. "He raised taxes on the plant, which forced them to downsize."

"Wait a minute," John stated. "Are we saying we don't believe this had anything to do with Dana and the Renfield murders?"

Quinn shook his head. "No, the timing is too co-incidental and I still think Dana was the target. Jessup was sitting behind her. If the shooter missed her, he would have hit the mayor. I think if we look into Bruce Davis's financials he's probably recently experienced a payoff. My guess is it's from the same person who is paying off Reed Jessup."

John nodded and turned to Rich and Quinn. "Go find Bruce Davis and bring him in for questioning. I'll run his financials. I'm tired of this game. I'm ready for answers."

Quinn nodded, but stopped to speak to his dad before he left. "Will you take Dana back to the station with you? I don't want to leave her alone."

"Sure. We'll be waiting." He put his hand on Quinn's shoulder and looked at them both. "Be careful."

"We will," Rich assured him.

Quinn walked back to the courthouse, where his brother's cruiser was still parked. Dana was waiting inside the courthouse for him, flanked by two armed deputies for her protection. She quickly ran outside to meet him as he approached the building.

"We have a lead on someone we believe might have been involved in this shooting. I'm going with Rich to bring him in. My father will take you back to the sheriff's office and keep you safe."

She nodded, but he sensed her fear beneath the surface. They would both feel better if he stayed with her, but like his dad, he was ready to end this game. He wanted to confront Bruce Davis before anything else happened. To end this once and for all, and possibly, set his sights on a life, a future with Dana.

"I'll be fine," he assured her, then kissed her long and hard as she clung to him before he broke it off. It was harder than he'd expected walking away from her, and he was sure this was how his teammates felt every time they left their loved ones to do the job.

He stopped at Rich's cruiser and readied himself for the upcoming confrontation by slipping on a protective vest and choosing a weapon. He was armed and ready for a physical confrontation, but as they got into the car and Rich started the engine, his words brought Quinn back to the emotional battle brewing inside of him.

"You have to tell her."

He stared out the window at the woman who had become so important to him in so little time and knew his brother was right. "I know." It was time to take a risk and pray his heart could handle the fallout.

Rich didn't bother with the siren as he pulled onto the land that belonged to Bruce Davis and his family.

"Keep your weapons low but ready," he advised Quinn, as if this was his first time. Rich often forgot Quinn had seen more battles than he had during his time with Delta and the SOA.

He parked and they quickly got out.

"We should have brought backup," Quinn stated, but Rich shook his head.

"I don't want to spook him." He knocked on the door, but they heard no movement from inside.

"Both cars are here," Quinn noted. He knew Bruce had a wife and family, so where were they?

They headed for the barn, moving cautiously and scanning for movement. Rich called out to Bruce, but again they heard nothing.

Quinn pushed open the barn door, raised his gun and scanned the area. He stopped and felt his heart drop when he spotted Bruce Davis hanging from a rope by a rafter. He was dead of an apparent suicide.

Dana tried to push back the feeling of disappointment when Quinn and his brother returned with news of Bruce Davis's death. It seemed they were blocked at every turn. Sheriff Dawson had already confirmed a large payout in the Davises' bank account and they were looking in to who had transferred that money into his account. Right now, they were operating on the assumption that whoever was pulling Reed Jessup's strings had also paid Bruce Davis to shoot Dana at the courthouse.

"What about Missy and the kids?" Clara asked when she learned about Bruce Davis's suicide.

Sheriff Dawson had found them, too. "He sent them to her mother's yesterday. They had no idea what he was planning to do."

"How awful for her," Clara stated.

Dana wanted to agree. She wanted to feel sorry for Missy Davis, but her husband had accepted money to try to kill her and sympathy was coming harder and harder for her. And they still didn't know who had paid off Bruce Davis.

Dana leaned into Quinn for comfort. She was growing so weary of this and ready for it to be over, but she was thankful he was still with her, supporting her.

"Maybe we should go back to the house and decompress for a while," he suggested and she was thankful for the offer. It was just what she wanted.

"That sounds good to me."

They went back to Quinn's house and settled into a comfortable silence. She focused on her work, searching online for other cold cases that might make good episodes for her show. Mason emailed her about the investigation in West Bend, asking about airing the case, but she nixed that idea. This investigation wasn't about ratings or programming. This was for her.

The longer she remained in West Bend, the more she began to wonder what it would have been like to have been raised here. If the murder hadn't happened, she would have lived in this town. She would have gone to school at West Bend High and possibly even met a teenaged Quinn during that time. She wondered if they would have liked each other. Would there have been the same attraction that she felt for him now, and would his protective nature have manifested itself then as well?

But Bill Mackey had ruined all that when he'd abandoned her.

She shook her head, pushing away such daydreams. This was her life and there was no sense in wondering about what might have been. It was what it was. And if she was going to focus on what-ifs, she could always start with her adoptive mom.

"What's that face for?" Quinn asked, sitting down beside her on the couch.

She tried to wave away his concern. "Nothing."

"No, tell me. What were you thinking about?"

She looked at him and smiled. She liked pretending they might have dated back in high school. "Actually, I was thinking about my mother, my adoptive mother."

"What was she like?"

"Driven. Ambitious. Distant." Dana sighed. She didn't often talk about her life. "My mother worked all the time. After my father passed away, she threw herself into her career as prosecutor. She was good at it, too. She had one of the highest conviction rates in the state and she had her eye on becoming district attorney one day. Instead, she got cancer and died."

"I'm sorry."

"I didn't even know I had been adopted until I found all that information when I was cleaning out her things. At first, I wondered why on earth she adopted me because she didn't seem to want to be a mother, but then I remembered the times before my dad died. I remember us being a family. I guess a part of her died when he did."

"How old were you when he passed away?"

"I was eleven. He went riding on his motorcycle one afternoon and never came home. The police pronounced it an accident and said he likely lost control and hit a tree."

"That sounds like a lonely way to grow up, Dana."

"It was." Loneliness had become her way of life ever since that day. She'd tried to fill that emptiness with others, relationships with men like Jason, and her career, but she'd never escaped that feeling of being abandoned. She hadn't understood it fully until she'd put the pieces together and realized her abandonment issues actually went much further back than she knew. Back to being a frightened one-year-old who'd been abandoned by a man who should have protected her.

He reached over and took her hand. "You're not alone anymore, Dana. You have me."

She stared into his face and wanted so badly to believe him, but she'd been burned too many times. Her heart cried out to her to be careful and not risk the pain of abandonment again. At least being alone meant no one could hurt you.

He pulled at her hand and locked eyes with her. "I mean it, Dana. I won't leave you." His green eyes were clear and free of hesitation. He really meant it, but she'd seen others mean it, too, until something happened that changed their minds.

He saw her hesitation and pulled her into his arms. "I'll have to prove it to you then. I was raised to be a man of my word."

Raised by the first person to abandon her.

She couldn't blame him for things his grandfather had done, but by his own admission, his grandfather had played a big part in making him the man he was. How could she trust her heart again after it had already been so broken and battered?

His phone rang and he pulled it out. "It's my dad." He pushed the speaker button on his phone. "Hey, Dad, what's up?"

"I just received a phone call from Colette Williams. Judge Henry signed the exhumation order on Alicia only. He'll sign the one for Rene if it turns out our suspicions are true and Alicia's grave is empty. We've got a crew heading to the cemetery right now. They'll take the casket to the coroner's office. Why don't you two meet us there?"

"We'll be there." Quinn hung up and turned to her, excitement written on his face.

Apprehension was all Dana felt. She should have been happy. This was the news she'd been waiting for and now that it was finally happening she felt sick instead. It was likely only nerves, but as Quinn got up and grabbed his keys, all she wanted to do was sit on this couch and forget that call had ever happened.

He kneeled beside her, his beautiful eyes glistening. He stroked her cheek, obviously sensing her hesitation. "This is what you've waited for. Let's go put this issue to rest once and for all."

She nodded and grabbed her purse and her phone. She couldn't allow nerves to get the better of her now. She was finally going to know the truth about whether or not Alicia Renfield died that night thirty years ago. She was finally going to know for certain who she was.

The waiting was the hardest part. Waiting for them to dig up the casket then haul it back to the coroner's office. Waiting for him to document and dictate and follow procedures line by line. It was frustrating to have the answer sitting right in front of him on a metal examination table in the laboratory and not be able to hurry along the reveal.

Quinn stayed beside Dana just as he'd promised her he would, but she seemed oddly calm given the circumstances. He chalked it up to nerves. Her entire life was about to change one way or another. Either she'd discover she'd been wrong about everything, or else she'd discover she'd been right and her life wasn't what she thought it was.

His life would change, too, if that casket was empty, because then he would finally know for sure that his grandfather had done something unimaginable by faking a little girl's death.

His father waved him and Dana into the room as they finished cutting open the seals on the tiny coffin. It broke his heart to see how small it was. A tiny coffin for a one-year-old. He'd known about this case all his life, but it had never hit home to him as it did at this moment.

The medical examiner ordered the seals removed and the latches opened.

He held his breath as his father lifted the lid. Dana reached for his hand and squeezed it. This was the moment she would know the truth one way or another. He looked at her and felt the anxiousness flowing off her.

"Well?" he demanded. Why were they keeping them in such suspense? "What do you see?"

The sheriff pushed the lid all the way open to reveal a satin interior, pink and delicate. But the coffin wasn't empty. His dad reached inside and pulled out one of several large stones lying where the body should have been.

"How could this have happened?" Quinn demanded. He couldn't say what he'd been expecting, but it hadn't been this. Part of him had believed Dana's story, but the other part hadn't been able to wrap his brain around the idea that his grandfather had faked the death of a child and left her abandoned sixty miles away.

His father turned to the coroner. "I'll speak with the prosecutor. Based on this new information, I believe she'll be able to persuade the judge to grant an exhumation order for Rene as well. They'll want to have the autopsy redone and its possible they may be able to obtain DNA." He spoke the last part to Dana as if that consolation should make up for what had been done to her.

All eyes in the room, including Quinn's, turned to look at Dana as the realization seemed to hit them all at the same time. They'd all bought into a thirty-year-old lie. Alicia Renfield hadn't died in the fire after all, as everyone believed. His grandfather and a handful of others had lied about her death. It was true. It was all true.

And someone had gone to great lengths to keep that truth from coming to light. Now their next step was to find out who…and why.

EIGHT

Mayor Jessup greeted Dana as she walked into his office. Quinn had insisted on bringing her and she was glad to have his support. She'd asked him to remain in the mayor's waiting room, but now she wished she'd brought him inside with her. She was surprised to find they weren't meeting alone. Two other people, one man and one woman, both dressed in suits, were also present and sitting beside the massive desk in the center of the room. She couldn't say what she had been expecting, but definitely something more personal now that everyone knew Alicia hadn't died the night of the fire. After all, Mayor Jessup had expressed an interest in speaking with her again if it turned out she was his daughter, and that was now an even greater possibility.

"Come in, come in," he said, getting up to greet her. He stuck out his hand for Dana to shake and she did so, but she noticed he seemed as stunned by this new development as everyone else she had spoken with since John Dawson had pulled rocks out of

Alicia Renfield's casket instead of a child. Beads of sweat were present on Mayor Jessup's forehead. He quickly wiped them away as he moved back around to his chair and motioned for Dana to take a seat.

"Dana, this is Walter Littlefield and Shirley Adams. Walter handles most of the city's legal issues and Shirley is my personal attorney. I asked them to be present while we spoke."

She wondered why he'd felt the need for lawyers but figured he was only covering himself and the city in case of any liability she might claim.

Mayor Jessup leaned back in his chair and shook his head. "I don't really know how to process this, if you want to know the truth. It's been a big day for us here in West Bend."

"For me as well," Dana told him.

He motioned to Shirley, who stood and approached her. "Being aware that you believe yourself to be Alicia Renfield, who supposedly died thirty years ago, we wanted to let you know that there no longer remains any property or money belonging to the estate of Paul and Rene Renfield. It was all seized by the county and used to cover taxes owed."

She couldn't stop the smile that spread across her face. They thought she was after the money from the estate. "I don't care about the money. I didn't come here for that."

"We felt you should know that before you proceeded with any legal actions. The property was purchased by Mayor Jessup's father-in-law and passed on to him and his wife in good faith that the legal heirs were all deceased."

"I understand."

She sat back down and the other one—Little-field—stood. "I'm glad to hear you're not concerned about receiving money from the estate. It seems a terrible injustice was perpetrated on you by former leaders of our community, but I hope you won't hold our little city accountable for the actions of only a few of its servants."

She saw where this was going. Mayor Jessup was worried first about his own pocketbook then about the city's. She addressed her comments to the mayor. "I have no plans to sue the city of West Bend at this time, but there is something I want from you, Mayor."

He stiffened. Gone was the sincere, concerned man she'd met in the sheriff's office. This was the rugged politician she was facing now. "What do you want, Miss Lang?"

She stood and leaned against his desk to drive home her point. "I want your nephew, Reed Jessup, captured before he hurts or kills anyone else."

He jumped to his feet. "Reed isn't a killer."

"If Deputy Jenkins dies, he is. He's in critical condition now and there is an entire library full of people who saw Reed chasing after me with a gun.

"Why would my nephew want you dead, Miss Lang?"

"Someone is paying him to prey on me, someone who never wanted this case to be reopened. Someone, I believe, who got away with murdering Rene Renfield thirty years ago. I intend to find out who and why, and I expect your nephew to pay for what he's done to me."

She turned and stormed out of his office. She was tired of playing games and she wasn't going to get caught up in one of Mayor Jessup's.

Quinn met her at the door as she exited the office. "I heard yelling. What did he want?"

"To protect his interests. He was worried I was going to try to stake some claim on the land that he owns."

"What did you tell him?"

"That I'd settle for his nephew locked in a jail cell."

He smiled and took her hand. "Why don't we take a walk." She followed him a few blocks, then he ducked under some trees and led her into a clearing. The trees surrounding the area created a mini garden hidden away from the city's traffic. It was complete with a creek, a waterfall and bench for sitting.

"It's beautiful," she said. "It's so peaceful here."

"We call this Winslow Gardens. I've wanted to bring you here before but it didn't seem like it was ever the right time."

He sat down on the bench and she took the spot beside him. He'd been strangely quiet ever since learning Alicia hadn't died, and it bothered her how distant he seemed. "Are you angry at me?" she finally asked him.

"No, why would I be?"

"It's because of me that people are talking about your grandfather. I don't know if maybe this changes the way you see him."

He leaned forward and sighed. "I don't know if it does. The man I knew... I never would have thought he would do something like this, but it seems he did. I don't really know how to process that. All I know is that I feel like I owe you an apology."

"No, you don't. You're not responsible for his actions. Besides, I'm not sure he meant it to harm me. I think he was trying to protect me." It didn't help ease the sting of abandonment she felt, but maybe someday it would. "Besides, Reed Jessup is still on the loose and I don't know who is behind all this." She entwined her hand in his. "I need you with me, Quinn, if you still want me."

He pulled her to him and wrapped his arms tightly around her, cocooning her into an embrace of protection and comfort. "I promised you I wasn't going to leave you, and I meant it. I don't blame you for any of this, Dana, and I hope once everything comes to light you won't ever doubt that again."

She laid her head on his chest and basked in his presence. She wouldn't have made it through any of this without him and she was thankful she didn't have to try.

"I have to tell her the truth," Quinn told his brother as they walked the perimeter of his home.

He'd made a promise that he would be there for her, and he'd meant it. He was falling for her and it didn't make any difference to him whether she was Alicia Renfield or Dana Lang. Her name wasn't as important to him as her beauty and passion and grace.

"Are you sure?" Rich asked him.

He nodded. "It's time."

He'd never been so certain of anything in his life. He wanted her to know all there was to know about him and that included his participation in the embassy rescue.

Somehow, this lady had managed to bring him back from the depths of despair, from questioning God and how his life had fallen apart to seeing a future that included her. He still missed his grandfather and Tommy, but she'd breathed new life into him and given him back his passion and zeal. He wanted something out of life again and that was all because of her doing.

He'd been hiding away, running home to lick his wounds because of all he'd lost. The double whammy of losing his beloved grandfather and then his best friend close together had taken with it his zeal for fighting. But now he could see coming home to someone like Dana waiting for him, finally having someone to put everything into perspective.

His world had changed. He saw a single star in the sky, but knew God saw so much more. He saw the galaxy. He saw every grain of sand on the beach, and He saw Quinn's life already lived. He knew the plans He had and what Quinn needed to do to get where he should be. Quinn didn't understand it, but he believed not in the circumstances of his life, but in its creator. Faith was and always had been the greatest ally he had, the most powerful weapon in his arsenal.

But lately, his faith had been sorely lacking. He'd been focusing on things of this world, like his own grief and loss, and blocking his heart from the pain of life again. Dana had changed all that. She'd pushed her way through all his boundaries, all the road blocks to his heart. She'd become important to him and he suddenly couldn't imagine a day without hearing her voice.

It was time to take a leap of faith with Dana.

Dana ran through some footage on her laptop. It was video for the next episode of *Newswatch* and according to her producer's email, it needed to be trimmed by a minute and a half. That was a lot of time and she was searching for some segment she could eliminate, but they all seemed important. But if she didn't find it, Mason would, and she would lose control of the content of the episode.

She jotted down several notes, possible places that could be trimmed by a few seconds. She had a list of up to thirty seconds when her pen ran out of ink. She shook it, hoping to jolt it back into working, but the ink was gone. She pulled open her purse and her briefcase and dug through each. She had to have an extra pen somewhere.

Not finding one, she looked around Quinn's living room for something to write with. She searched through the kitchen hoping he had a secret stash of ink pens, but she didn't find one. Finally, she searched through a console in the living room and stumbled across one at the bottom of the drawer. She pulled out several things, including a framed photograph, so she could get to it. While replacing the items, she glanced at the photo and felt her heart stop beating.

She recognized the man standing arm in arm with Quinn. Tommy Woods, one of the two operatives who'd died in the attack on the embassy. His face had been plastered all over the news in the six weeks since the attack.

And here was a photograph of Quinn with him, arm in arm, hidden inside a drawer.

Had they served together? It was unlikely. Woods had been a Navy Seal, not a Delta operator. The two men might have gone on missions together during combined missions, but the two elite Special Forces groups rarely worked together. How then had Quinn come to know Tommy Woods well enough to pose for a photo and take the time to frame it?

Neither man in the picture was in uniform and both had beards and shaggy hair. They wore desert attire and the landscape behind them was clearly some overseas location. She pinched the bridge of her nose as realization hit her. Quinn had the skills and background the CIA recruited for special security, and he knew one of the men who'd died in the embassy attack. Add to that the fact that he was secretive with his background around her and she knew the truth.

She took a deep breath, then let it out slowly. She'd been spending time with one of the operatives from the attack. No wonder he'd been secretive about his job. He was used to not revealing the details. It was a habit that was deeply ingrained in him from his time with Delta. She remembered how difficult it was to get Rizzo to open up about his experiences during the attack.

Suddenly, the weight of what she'd just realized hit her. Quinn knew Rizzo. Had worked and fought with him during the embassy attack. He had to know she'd interviewed Rizzo about his experience. Had he kept this secret from her because of her reporter status? Did he never intend to tell her? Anger bit at her for foolishly believing they'd gotten closer than that.

She fumed about it until she heard Quinn's car pull up. She'd been through a range of emotions while waiting for him—anger, indignation, understanding and anger again. He entered the house whistling and she saw happiness written across his face. Their relationship had taken a turn recently and she hated to send it two steps backward, but she couldn't ignore the truth, either. He hadn't trusted her enough to tell her the truth about himself.

"I found this where you were trying to hide it from me." She handed him the photograph and watched as he realized what it was and its significance. "You're a contract security operative for the CIA, aren't you? And you were a part of the team that responded to the embassy attack."

He looked at her, green eyes probing her face for

understanding. "I was coming in here to tell you about this."

"That's pretty convenient, Quinn."

"It's the truth. I told Rich I wanted you to know."

"Sure, you wanted me to know. That's why you hid this picture from me and changed the subject every time I asked about your job or your time in the military." She hated the sarcastic tone of her voice, but she also hated the mistrust that flowed through her. It turned out he was another person in her life to let her down. Hot tears pressed the back of her eyes. "I shared my most private secret with you, but you didn't care enough about me to do the same." She turned away from him as a tear slid down her face.

"I wanted to trust you with this, Dana, but I didn't know if I could. You are a reporter and you told me yourself that you would kill to find out the identities of Rizzo's teammates."

She remembered uttering those words but she hadn't meant them. Not really. There were lines she wouldn't cross, and outing Quinn as one of Rizzo's teammates was a big one. But he didn't believe that. He still saw her as a reporter first and a woman second.

"I got worried. Naming me means an end to my career. What will I do then? Come back home and join the sheriff's office and catch speeders out on route seven for the rest of my life? I'm trained to catch terrorists."

She pushed back the tears that threatened to overtake her. "I didn't seek Rizzo out. He came to me.

He wanted to tell his story. I won't deny that it was a boost to my career to be the one to break it. It was. But, Quinn, you have to know that I would never betray your trust over a story. In fact, I would never betray your trust period. You took a risk getting close to me and all the while thinking that I might destroy your life with one phone call. I wouldn't." Her anger dissipated and now all she wanted was for him to believe her. She grabbed his arm and forced him to turn to face her. She placed her hands on his face. Nothing was more important to her than making him believe this. Nothing.

"I would never betray your trust, Quinn. You never have to be afraid to share something with me. I promise you that anything you tell me in confidence will remain with me forever. Don't you know I'm completely crazy about you?"

A slow smile spread across his face and he covered her hand with his. "Really? You're crazy about me?"

A sense of relief rushed through her at his light-hearted comment. Hopefully, now all the barriers between them were gone. "Completely."

"I'm glad you know," he whispered in her ear. "You told me your secrets and now you know mine. And I trust you, Dana. I trust you completely."

She leaned in and kissed him and he tightened his arms around her. It was the only place she wanted to be.

The next morning, Quinn went outside to clear his head. He stayed close to the house, but the fresh air helped him put things in perspective. He'd meant it when he'd told Dana he was glad she knew about him working for the SOA. He wanted her to know everything there was about his life. After all, if he couldn't trust the woman he'd fallen in love with, who could he trust?

He stopped to catch his breath. He'd used the *L* word and he wasn't afraid of it. He loved her. There was no use denying it. He'd fallen head over heels for the beautiful Dana Lang and was already imagining a future that included her. It seemed that after a long, dark period of his life, God was finally working things out his way.

He went back inside. After showering, he turned on the coffeemaker and listened to the slow, steady drip into the pot. His phone buzzed and he scooped it up. It was his brother.

"Morning, Rich."

"Did you tell her?" His brother's voice held tension and anger.

"What?"

"Did you tell Dana last night about being a covert security operative for the CIA."

Something was wrong. He felt it in Rich's tone. "I told her. Why?"

Rich grunted. "Turn on the TV, Quinn. Your name and face are breaking news this morning."

He stiffened and walked into the living room. This felt like a dream and one he didn't care to continue in. He picked up the remote and turned on the TV. "What station?"

"All of them."

His heart stopped when he realized his brother was correct. The news had broken into regular programming to report his information. His military photograph was in the top right corner of the screen and the scroll at the bottom was all about him being a part of the embassy rescue team.

He was paralyzed in place, unable to move, unable to even adjust the volume. His greatest fear had come true. Only a few minutes ago, his life had seemed right on track. Now, it was crashing down all around him.

"I can't believe she did that to you after all you've done for her." His brother's reaction was full of anger and bitterness, but all Quinn could muster was shock and disappointment. He wouldn't have believed it if it wasn't staring him right in the face.

Dana emerged from the spare bedroom already dressed for the day. "Good morning." She walked over and poured herself a cup of coffee.

"Do you want me to come over there?" Rich asked. "I've got a thing or two to say to her myself."

"No," Quinn said. "Don't come over." He hung up with his brother and turned to Dana, who stood in the kitchen fixing her coffee. She looked happy and innocent…as if she hadn't just stabbed him in the back.

"Who was that? Your brother?"

He moved so he wasn't blocking the television. She glanced at the screen, then dropped her mug and cupped her hands over her mouth in shock. She listened as the anchor related that the information had been listed on *Newswatch's* website, along with the promise of an exclusive interview to come. She looked at him and fear flittered through her eyes, fear that he blamed her.

He did.

"Quinn, I'm so sorry. What can I do? There has to be something I can do to fix this."

There was nothing she could do. There was nothing anyone could do. His face was plastered across the TV, across the nation. His career was over. With one phone call or email to her producer, she'd burned him.

"Wait, you can't think I had anything to do with this, can you? I didn't. I promise I didn't."

"I'll call my dad and have someone else come watch the house. I can't stay here. I have to leave."

He headed for the door, but she grabbed his arm and spun him to face her. "Quinn, I promise you that this was not my doing."

"I confided in you, Dana." He scooped up his keys and marched out the door.

She could play the innocent victim in this matter, but it didn't make one bit of difference. His career as a security operator overseas was over.

Dana watched him climb into his car and speed away. She walked back inside. The newscaster was repeating the breaking news of another operative identified. She picked up the remote and clicked it off. Seeing it had been like a punch to her stomach. She could only imagine how it had felt to Quinn.

It was true. His career was ruined. He could never go incognito overseas again when everyone in the world had seen his image on TV.

She hadn't told anyone what he'd told her in confidence, but she had a sickening feeling that she was indeed to blame for it. She picked up her phone and dialed Tracy's number.

"I saw the news," she said when her friend answered. "What happened?"

"I know you said not to look into this guy, Dana, but I couldn't have my friend around some weirdo, could I? Besides, can you believe you were sitting on top of such a huge news story?" She was excited about this revelation and her part in breaking this story. Dana could hear it all in her voice.

But she wasn't in the mood to celebrate. "How could you do this to me, Tracy?"

"Don't worry. I gave you credit for the find. I tried to call you several times but you didn't answer so Mason said to run with it."

Dana glanced at her phone and saw several missed calls from Tracy yesterday. She'd been too busy dealing with the exhumation that she hadn't returned them.

"And yes, every other journalist in town is green with envy. You were right. Feathers are being ruffled."

She didn't want credit. She wanted to scream and holler and cry that her friend had ruined everything. "Don't you realize what you've done? You've ruined this man's livelihood. He'll never be able to work special ops again."

Tracy grew serious. "I thought this was what you wanted. You were the one pushing for the interview with Rizzo. I thought I was doing you a favor."

She recalled Quinn's horror-stricken face as he stared at the TV. "I didn't want this," she said. But she couldn't really blame her friend, could she? It had been her ambition and her determination that Tracy had been following. A week ago, she would have jumped on this story and hounded Quinn for an interview. But she wasn't the same person now that she was one week ago.

"Dana, I'm sorry. I was only doing what I thought you'd want." Her friend sounded genuinely sorry and Dana knew she had no idea why she was apologizing.

"I know you meant well, but I think you cost me something amazing."

She hung up with Tracy and went out to stand on the porch. She took in the landscape and how beautiful it was here, but it was all ruined for her now. She wanted to scream out in pain and frustration. Where was Quinn's God now when his life had been turned upside down because of her? Tears pressed against her eyes but she pushed them back. She deserved this. She'd gotten too close to Quinn and destroyed his life. It was no wonder she could never find happiness. She was truly unlovable, but this time instead of only her getting hurt, she was now including others in her pain.

Her phoned buzzed inside and she hurried back

in to grab it. Maybe it was Quinn calling. But as she swooped her phone from the coffee table, she realized the futility of her high hopes. She glanced at the caller ID and didn't recognize the number. She wiped away a tear that slipped through. She wasn't in the mood to have a conversation with someone she didn't even know. She pushed the button to send the caller to voice mail, set her phone back on the coffee table, then dropped onto the couch.

She had to come up with some way to get them both out of this mess even though it seemed impossible.

Her phone dinged, this time indicating a text message. She pushed away the hope that it was Quinn but glanced at the screen just in case. It wasn't him, but the message did catch her attention. It was from the same number she'd sent to voice mail.

I thought you wanted to talk. JE

She sat up, realizing those initials belonged to Jay Englin. And she had listed her phone number in an email she'd sent to several old email addresses she'd found for him.

Her phone rang again and this time, she snapped it up. "Hello."

"I understand you've been trying to find me."

Her heart jumped into her throat. Was this really Jay Englin on the phone with her? The only man left who could answer her questions? "Who is this?" she demanded, guarding her enthusiasm.

"You know who I am. I know you have questions. I have the answers you're seeking. Meet me at Winslow Gardens in an hour. I'll answer all your questions."

He hung up without giving her an opportunity to question him further. She didn't want to go without Quinn. Her logical side knew this might be a trap, but she couldn't ignore it. What if it wasn't? What if it really was Jay Englin and she blew him off? She couldn't live with not knowing.

She quickly dialed Quinn's cell phone, but the call went straight to voice mail. She groaned, angry at his childish response. He might be done with her, but he could at least take her call. She wanted to scream at him, but most of all, she wanted him by her side.

She didn't have time to wait for Quinn to get over his anger and decide to speak with her. By the time he did, Jay might be gone and with him all the answers to her questions. She called Quinn's number again as she grabbed the keys to her car and hurried outside. It went right to voice mail again, but this time she left a message.

"Quinn, it's Dana. I received a phone call from Jay Englin. I'm meeting him at Winslow Gardens. Please come. I know you're mad and I can't blame you, but I really don't want to be alone." There was much more she wanted to say to him, to apologize and explain that she hadn't meant to plant the seed in Tracy's head to out him, but now wasn't the time and she didn't want to ask forgiveness on his voice mail.

She waited for the phone to ring as she drove, but by the time she reached Winslow Gardens, it still hadn't.

She wondered if he'd even heard her message. He'd probably seen it was her calling and decided not to bother.

Suddenly, a voice inside of her warned her away. She shouldn't be here alone meeting someone she couldn't even be sure was Jay Englin. This was most likely a trap and she was walking right into it. She spotted movement in the trees and a figure motioning to her and knew she was going to go despite her fears. It was a risk she had to take.

Where are you, Quinn?

He ended up at his parents' house, on their couch, his face covered by his arm. His life was in shambles and it was all his fault for believing that Dana was a woman first and a reporter second.

"What have I done? I can't believe I ever trusted her."

His mother sat beside him and stroked his arm. "You've always been a risk taker. You follow your instincts and they told you she could be trusted."

"My instincts were wrong."

His dad interjected. "Your instincts are rarely wrong, Quinn. I think you're overanalyzing this. It's obvious to everyone else that Dana cares for you and you for her. I find it hard to believe she would betray you this way."

"Then how do you explain it? My face, my name plastered all over the television?"

"I don't have an explanation. You'll have to get that from her. What did she have to say about it?"

"I don't know. I was angry, and I stormed out before she could explain anything. I didn't want to hear her excuses. No one else knew about my involvement. It had to come from her."

"That's not entirely true. We have an entire town that has some clue about what you've been doing. We were pretty worried about you when the news about the embassy attack came across the wire. It was no secret around town that you were involved. People dropped in to pray with us or bring food by."

His mom nodded. "That's true."

He sat up. He knew that was true. Even Mayor Jessup, who he hardly knew, had commented on the embassy attack. "You think someone in town ratted me out to the news stations?"

His dad shrugged. "You've been ruffling a lot of feathers with this Renfield investigation. Maybe you ruffled the wrong one and that person decided to keep you otherwise occupied with this. I mean, it's worked, hasn't it? You're not thinking about the Renfield murders and you're not even on speaking terms with Dana."

His dad was right. He'd fallen into the trap. "You think so?"

"What I think is that you need to talk to Dana. Give her an opportunity to defend herself and you have to really listen. This is done. There's no taking it back, Quinn, but what you and Dana have started here is important. You can't let it go or else a murderer wins. They've already gotten away with this for thirty years. Don't let them win again."

His parents both stood and left him alone to ponder his decision. He knew they were right. He at least owed it to Dana to listen to her explanation.

She'd claimed to have no idea how his name had been linked to the embassy attack and she had seemed as surprised as he was. Had he jumped the gun? Allowed his anger to overshadow everything else?

And fear. He'd fallen back on his fear of being hurt. He'd been expecting it and he was ready when he thought it had happened. He'd gotten close to her, fallen hard for her, but had never really trusted her.

He jumped to his feet and headed for the door. He had to talk to her.

She got out of the car and walked under the overhanging branches. A trickle of water greeted her ears as did the chirp of the crickets. Again, she sensed this wasn't a good idea, but it was too late. She was here and would see this through to the end.

A figure approached from the trees, and she recognized the tall, thin man from the newspaper articles she'd seen proclaiming him a reluctant hero for finding Alicia. His hair was now grey and the lines around his eyes accentuated his increased age.

"It's only me," he said. "You're Dana Lang?"

She nodded and he stepped closer, giving her a full view of him now. He appeared to be a middle-aged man in his fifties with blond hair greying at the temples and a full beard. Yet he was slim and fit, a man who took care of himself. "I'm Jay Englin."

She was so stunned to actually be talking to him that for a moment she couldn't form any words. Finally, she held out her hand to him. "Thank you for responding to my email. I never expected you would come to town, but I'm glad you did."

"I shouldn't have, but I felt you deserved answers after all these years. I've kept up with you through the years, watched you grow, made certain you were safe."

Suddenly, she was creeped out to know this man had been following her for years. She took a step backward from him. "What do you mean you've been watching me?"

"I only meant—" He gave her a sharp look. "You're an investigative journalist. I thought you would have figured it all out by now."

"That I'm Alicia Renfield? Yes, I have, but how do you know who I am?"

"Because I'm the one who left you at that church thirty years ago. We had to make sure you were safe. After that, I followed your journey to being adopted. When I saw your first piece on television, I recognized your new name."

"But why did you leave me there? Why did you want everyone to believe I was dead? Do you know what happened to my father and who killed my mother?"

"I'm sorry. I don't know, but Sheriff Mackey never believed Paul killed his wife. He always thought Paul was probably dead. Bill thought you would be safer if people believed you were dead, but none of us ever thought it would take this long to solve the case."

"But how did I survive the fire?"

"You were never in the fire, Dana. The Mackeys were babysitting you that night. Rene had brought you over to them an hour earlier. They were going to keep you for the weekend so she and Paul could have a romantic weekend. I was shocked when I arrived at their house and saw the baby playing on the floor."

She pushed a frustrated hand through her hair. "I don't understand. Why keep my being alive a secret? Why the need to fake my death?"

"Bill figured out pretty quickly that Paul wasn't the killer. He suspected Jessup. He and Rene used to be an item and she'd confided in him that Jessup had gotten obsessed with her. He was always calling and accidentally running in to her. Some people in town even suspected that you were his child. Bill thought if he discovered you were alive, he might try to kill you again. The accelerant that was used to ignite the house was found upstairs in the hallway by your nursery, meaning that whoever set that fire intended for you to die in it as well. He thought you would be safer. Bill knew the preacher and I took you there and gave you to him."

How ironic. She'd felt alone all her life, her abandonment only the beginning of a lifelong struggle with loneliness even if she hadn't known its origins.

"You may think the sheriff didn't do the right thing, but you'd be wrong. When we started trying to look in to the case, attempts were made on my life. Bill's life was in danger, too. I finally left town hoping it would quiet down. I've tried to stay under the radar all these years because I feared for my life if whoever committed those murders found out what I knew and what I'd done."

As if to punctuate his fears, a shot rang out. She

jumped and spun around. When she turned back to Jay, he had an odd look on his face. He grabbed his chest and only then did she notice blood pooling on his shirt. He fell to the ground and she ran to him.

He grabbed her arm and dug into it, struggling to say his final word. "Run!" he softly yelled before he fell back and closed his eyes.

Dana grabbed him and tried to wake him but she knew it was too late. He was dead. He was right about his life being at risk. He'd returned to West Bend after all these years only to finally be killed.

Who would do this? And who had even known Jay was back in town?

She heard footsteps and glanced up. Reed Jessup was running toward her, gun raised. She leaped to her feet and bolted into the brush, but she wasn't quick enough. Dana screamed as he grabbed her from behind and tossed her to the ground. She landed hard on a rock, hitting her head. Blood splattered and a sick feeling rushed through her as her head began to swim.

Her arms and legs refused to move, making escape impossible. Blood ran into her face and the world seemed to fade. This was it. She was going to die.

But instead of shooting her, Reed put away his gun and lifted her, heaving her over his shoulder.

"Why are you doing this?" she asked him.

"Someone wants to have a few words with you before I kill you," he responded.

She knew what was happening but she was helpless to stop it. All she could do was give a little cry as she lost consciousness.

NINE

His first indication that something was wrong was that Dana's rental car was gone. He pulled up to the house and got out, quickly going inside. His pulse kicked up a notch when he saw she wasn't there. He checked each room but she was gone. He also noticed her cell phone and purse were missing.

He pulled out his phone to call her and saw he had two missed voice mails, one from her and one from his brother. He checked the volume and realized his phone was on silent. He'd missed both the calls and the voice mail notifications. His gut clenched as he listened to her message. How could she do something as reckless as going to meet a stranger alone? With guilt, he realized he'd placed her in that situation by walking out on her.

He dialed her number. It rang several times then flipped over to voice mail. "Dana, it's Quinn. Call me. Let me know you're okay."

He listened to Rich's message and learned the deputy he'd sent over to watch Dana had left when he'd seen no one was home.

Quinn picked up his rifle then grabbed his keys and walked back to his car. He headed for Winslow Gardens, continuing to try her phone as he drove. Each time, it went to voice mail. If anything happened to her, he didn't know how he would handle it.

He made it to Winslow Gardens, pulling up beside her car, which was still parked there. He glanced inside—the car was empty and her purse and phone were gone. He didn't see another car. Whoever she was meeting must have already left or else hadn't driven. Pushing through the brush, he called to her, but received no response and the clearing was empty.

A hundred terrible images flashed through his mind of things that might have happened to her. He tried her phone again, but this time, he heard a ringing when he called it. He followed the sound and discovered her cell phone lying in the grass. She wouldn't have left it behind on purpose.

He scanned the area and spotted a figure on the ground behind the bench. His heart stopped as he panicked, wondering if it was Dana lying there and what he would do if it was. As he moved closer, he saw it wasn't her. The figure was too large to be Dana and the hair was blond instead of her dark brunette.

He pulled his gun then moved toward what he realized was a male figure. He aimed his gun at the figure then bent down to turn him over. He didn't recognize the man. Was this the guy Dana had said she was meeting? Jay Englin?

Whoever it was, he was dead from what looked like a gunshot to the chest.

And Dana was nowhere to be found.

Quinn watched his brother process the murder scene, then have the body of Jay Englin moved. A small crowd had gathered near the park and the police were questioning onlookers about what they might have seen.

He stayed on the periphery of the scene. He'd told them all he knew about Dana's supposed meeting with Jay Englin. The man on the ground was approximately the right age as Englin would be now and faintly resembled the photo Dana had cut out from the newspaper clippings of the man who'd been described as finding little Alicia Renfield in the rubble of the fire. This man had lighter hair and a full beard, but he'd been so hard to find that it wasn't unlikely to believe he'd changed his appearance to remain underground.

Quinn's father was standing a few feet away on the phone. He hung up and turned to Quinn. "One of the techs did in-field fingerprinting on the body and sent it back to the station. Our victim has been confirmed as Jay Englin. His prints were on file in our system because of his former employment. I also had a computer tech dig through Dana's phone records. She did receive a phone call from an unknown number. The call lasted several minutes."

"Long enough to arrange a meeting with Englin," Quinn stated and his father agreed.

Quinn hated to think about Dana struggling with a killer, but she was nowhere to be found. Something must have happened to her. Given her cell phone's placement, it had probably fallen out during a struggle. He stood and faced his father. "I'm going back to the station to see what I can do to track down Reed Jessup."

His father shook his head. "We've flagged his known phone and bank accounts and have a BOLO out on his vehicle. It's registered to the Jessups, but so far it hasn't been found. He has no known address but we've got deputies searching known drug havens."

Quinn ran a hand over his face. His father and brother were doing everything they could to help him, but it seemed they were no closer to tracking down Reed Jessup, and finding Dana, than they'd been before. "I can't stand here," he said. "I have to do something."

"Like what?"

"I'm going to talk to the Jessups again. Maybe they've heard from Reed."

His father nodded. "I'll come with you. Rich, you're in charge of finishing up here."

Quinn walked off and slid into the passenger side of his father's car. He was anxious and feeling dread, fearing that something terrible had happened to Dana. Whoever had shot and killed Englin was trying to shut up everyone who knew anything about the Renfield case, and Dana was the smoking gun that could finally bring their crime to light.

His father tapped his shoulder. "It's going to be okay," he said. "We'll find her."

Quinn wanted to believe him, hoped he was right, but his greatest fear was that the longer it took them to track her down, the more likely they'd already be too late.

His phone beeped as they were getting into the car. Quinn glanced at an email he'd received in response to an alert about money transferred into Bruce Davis's account. Finally, he had an answer to his questions.

"What is it?" his dad asked him.

Quinn sighed. "I think you need to call Mayor Jessup and have him meet us at the sheriff's office immediately."

The hardness of the surface she was lying on was the first thing Dana noticed as she awoke. The second was the chill in the air and the dampness of the concrete floor. Pain shot through her head, causing her to groan. She tried to pull her hand to her head but discovered it was bound behind her.

She jerked awake at this realization and found herself sitting on the floor of an old building with one open wall. She glanced around and saw old farm equipment covered in dust that looked as if it hadn't been moved in years and what looked to be an old well pump several inches from her. She had no idea where she was, but slowly the memory of being attacked returned to her. Fear gripped her as a figure stepped into view. Reed Jessup had shot and killed Jay Englin and kidnapped her.

Only it wasn't Reed that entered the room.

She gasped as a female figure appeared before her. The woman had her hair and makeup done as if she had arrived for a party instead of a kidnapping.

She kneeled beside Dana. "Do you know who I am?"

Dana nodded. She recognized this woman right down to the pantsuit that had had blood all over it the last time they'd been together. "Meredith Jessup."

"That's right."

"Why do you have me tied up? Why did you bring me here?"

"I thought we should have a chat before the unpleasantries."

Unpleasantries. Is that what she called cold-blooded murder? "What do you want with me?" She couldn't imagine a scenario where Meredith Jessup had anything against her.

"That Bill Mackey pulled one over on us, didn't he? I heard the news that Alicia's grave was empty. Little Alicia didn't die in the fire that night at all, did she? I should have known. Rene said the child was sleeping upstairs, but I never heard a peep out of her."

Dana's blood ran cold and dread filled her. "You were there the night Rene died? You were inside the house?"

Dana pulled at the binding on her hands as another person entered the room. Reed Jessup. Dread settled in the pit of her stomach. She was going to die here tonight. And it turned out it was all because of Calvin Jessup's obsession with Rene. But she wouldn't grovel or beg for her life. She wouldn't give Meredith the pleasure of seeing that. "That's why my mother had to die? Because your fiancé got cold feet?"

"No. She had to die for the same reason you should have thirty years ago. I won't have a child of Calvin's and Rene's walking this earth. He's mine. Do you understand me? He's always been mine."

She saw the bitterness in Meredith's hard, cold eyes. She believed Dana was her husband's child, and she'd thought she took care of the problem thirty years ago only to discover she hadn't. Dana pulled at the tape on her wrists. Quinn's grandfather was right to hide her. It turned out she was in fact in great danger. "The police already know Reed was involved. This will eventually trace back to you."

"I've made arrangements for Reed. I've turned to him time and again this past week and each time he's failed me. This time, I intend to make certain it's done."

She pulled out a gun, then stood and turned to Reed, shooting him several times in the chest. He looked stunned as he fell to the floor, his eyes full of wonder and shock.

"You're pathetic," she told him as he stared up at her with a stunned expression. "You're pathetic and weak and no longer of any use to me." She fired again, this time shooting him in the head and leaving no doubt he was dead.

Meredith coldly slipped the gun back into her pocket. "Don't go anywhere," she said sarcastically to Dana as she disappeared.

Dana knew she had to get loose before Meredith returned. She'd proven herself capable of murder and if she would murder the man she'd raised like a son, she would have no qualms about killing her.

Panic gripped her when Meredith came back in with a shovel and a roll of plastic.

Dana jerked away. "What are you going to do with that?" She didn't really want to know but the question came flowing from her.

Her heart cried out for Quinn. Was he even looking for her? He probably didn't even know she was missing yet. Why hadn't she phoned him and apologized? She hadn't betrayed him. She should have tried harder to convince him of that. More importantly, she should have told him that she'd fallen in love with him and wanted to spend her life with him. But no, she'd let him walk away. She'd allowed him to blame her and push her away.

Now she realized with horror that she would never see him again. He would always blame her for outing him as an operative and worst of all, he would always doubt her love for him.

Oh, God, don't let this be the end. Don't let him suffer that way.

No matter what happened to her tonight, all she wanted for Quinn was happiness and a good life. If it couldn't be with her, then she prayed he would find someone else to love and not continue to remain alone.

Tears rolled down her eyes. She was surely about to die and all her thoughts were of Quinn. She longed for one last moment in his arms that made her feel safe and loved, one last kiss, one last second of pure belonging that she'd finally found in him.

She'd gone searching for family and found more than she'd ever expected. She'd found not only her true family, the Renfields, but also a family she wanted to belong to. Now she would pay the price for her curiosity. She would die as she should have thirty years ago.

Why, God? Why did You allow this to happen to me? Why did You let me find Quinn only to lose him now? Why did You dangle a family and happiness in front of me only to have it yanked away? It isn't fair! It isn't fair! She wanted to scream it at the top of her lungs. What kind of God allowed such evil to win?

Meredith picked up the shovel and turned to her. "Now to take care of you once and for all."

She used the shovel to pry off the lid of what looked like an old well. Dana assumed it was an old water well, given the pump. It must have been closed off years ago. Meredith managed to push the lid off and create a large opening—large enough for Dana to disappear into.

The woman meant to bury her alive!

Dana shrieked in terror, but Meredith only laughed in response.

"Go ahead and scream all you want, Miss Lang.

No one will hear you out here. This is all private land and no one has lived here in years." She picked up the shovel and held it out, ready to use it as a weapon.

Dana stared into Meredith's eyes and saw nothing but coldness. This woman had no qualms about what she was about to do. She had no hesitation about taking a life and then returning to her own life as if nothing had happened.

Dana faced the truth as Meredith swung the shovel at her head. She was going to die tonight.

TEN

"Are you kidding me?" Mayor Jessup asked as he looked over the paper Quinn had shown him about the money transfer. "How certain is this?"

Quinn leaned against the interview table. "It's very certain. The money that was transferred into Bruce Davis's account to pay for him shooting into the courthouse, shooting you, Mayor, came from your wife's private account. She's been paying Reed to do her dirty work. She must have gotten desperate and sloppy with Bruce. She left a paper trail."

"I don't understand." He fell into the chair. "Why would Meredith pay someone to shoot me?"

"I'm not so sure she did. I still believe Bruce was trying to hit Dana."

He shook his head. "No, Meredith would never harm Dana. She's family. She's my family."

"How did your wife feel about discovering you had a daughter come back from the dead?" Quinn asked him.

"We'll, she wasn't crazy about it, but she would

have gotten used to the situation." He seemed like he was grasping for hope, but didn't truly believe it himself. He looked up at Quinn. "She was always so jealous of anyone. She didn't even like Reed coming to live with us in the beginning because she felt it demeaned her for not being able to have kids of her own. But she grew to care for Reed like a son. I thought maybe something similar would happen with Dana eventually."

"Where is she now, Mayor?" Quinn felt it in his gut that Meredith Jessup was behind everything. She'd never struck him as a particularly easy person to get along with, but he knew jealousy was a powerful motivator. Plus, it made sense that Reed would trust his own aunt enough to do her bidding. Had she also been the one to shoot Rene and start the fire that Jessup had spent his lifetime being accused of?

Jessup shook his head. "I have no idea. I haven't seen her since this morning."

Quinn felt like they were going in circles. Jessup knew surprisingly little about his wife's activities. He didn't know if that was normal in a marriage, but it didn't make any sense to him.

The door opened and his father entered. "We found her," he stated. "Montgomery is bringing her in."

"What's going to happen to her?" Jessup asked.

"She'll be arrested for hiring a man to shoot you and then we'll demand some answers about Dana."

Jessup shook his head and stood. "She won't answer them. She's too clever for that. Her first response will be to ask for a lawyer."

"What do you suggest?" Quinn asked him.

"Bring her in here. Let me talk to her."

Quinn glanced at his father. Should they allow Jessup to talk to her? And if they did, would the pair work out a story that would explain everything away?

"Dana is in danger," the mayor said, looking to Quinn. "She's my daughter and I don't want to see anything happen to her. I can get Meredith to tell me where she is."

His dad motioned him outside and Quinn went. "What do you think?" the sheriff asked.

It was a big risk letting their two best suspects into a room together, but Quinn tended to believe Jessup. "I don't think he has any clue what his wife and nephew have been up to."

His dad agreed. "It's worth a shot."

They both turned as they heard a woman's voice demanding to know what was happening as she was led through the department. Quinn recognized her as Meredith Jessup.

He watched as his dad went to intercept her and led her into the room where her husband remained. Quinn turned on the intercom and listened and watched as the couple confronted one another.

"Calvin, what's happening? Why am I being arrested?"

He stood and approached her, but instead of comforting her, he broke into accusations. "Did you pay someone to shoot me, Meredith? Are you so unhappy here that you would pay a man to kill me?"

That accusation got a rise out of her. "Of course I didn't. You were never in danger. I was doing damage control, Calvin. Don't you see that? These people are trying to rope you back into that murder scandal. I only hired Davis to wound you so it would steer suspicion away from you."

The mayor didn't even flinch when she admitted to hiring Davis to shoot him.

"I didn't have anything to do with Rene's death. I don't need you steering suspicion away from me for anything and I don't need damage control."

"Of course you do. Everything I've ever done has been about advancing your career, but you're just as happy to stay here in West Bend and play mayor, aren't you? You don't even care that that woman's arrival could mean the end of your bid for senator, do you?"

"That woman is my daughter."

"Stop saying that," Meredith shrieked. "She is not and will never be your daughter. You're mine, Calvin. I made sure of that thirty years ago and I'll make sure of it again."

She stopped and gasped, seeming to realize what she'd said and, worse, who she'd said it in front of.

"What have you done, Meredith?"

She folded her arms and clammed up. "I'm not saying another word."

But she didn't need to. Quinn opened the door and stepped inside. "You just admitted to hiring a man to shoot into a courthouse and wound your husband. How do you think your husband's political career will handle a jailbird for a wife?"

Jessup took another step toward her. "Meredith, where is Dana? Have you done something to harm her?"

She looked at him and smiled a cold, hard smile. "She's someplace she'll never hurt us again."

Jessup turned to Quinn. "I know that look. She won't talk."

"I guess you do know me after all, Calvin. I won't say another word without my lawyer present."

Jessup's face lit up. "GPS. Her car has GPS. I'll call the company and find out where she's been all day." He reached for his phone and dialed the number as Quinn's father stepped inside to read Meredith Jessup her rights under the law and handcuff her.

Quinn looked into her face and saw nothing but hardness underneath her perfectly coifed makeup and fancy clothes. This was a woman who'd fought hard for what she had and wouldn't give up fighting.

He could imagine the scenario all those years ago. Her soon-to-be husband, the man she'd attached her future to, breaking off their engagement to marry another woman. Even back then, as a young woman, she hadn't been able to stand not getting her way.

"You killed her, didn't you? You killed Rene and tried to kill her daughter, too."

She gazed at him then spoke her final words on the matter. "I fought for what was mine."

Mayor Jessup hurried back over. "They gave me

an address for the last place her car was today. I recognize it. It's the old Renfield estate. Reed must have
taken Dana there."

It made perfect sense in a Meredith Jessup kind
of world. It would all end in the same place it had
begun. But Quinn couldn't leave her without issu-
ing one last warning.

"You'd better hope your nephew hasn't done anything to harm Dana, Mrs. Jessup."

Quinn hurried from the department and hopped
into the car, this time sliding into the driver's seat.
His father didn't follow him so he took off. His mind
was racing at all the things Reed had already tried
to do to Dana. He prayed he wasn't too late to save
her. He gripped the steering wheel as he barreled
through town toward the Renfield place.

*Lord, I don't think I can handle another loss.
Please don't let me lose her, too.*

He'd lost so much already. Tommy's death had
sent his life reeling out of control. How would he
react to losing someone else he cared about? And
he did care about her. He loved her, and he'd never
even told her. Anger bit at him as he realized she
might die without ever knowing that. The last thing
she would know from him was him walking out the
door, abandoning her as everyone else in her life had
done, and as he'd promised never to do.

Dana's head was pounding as she slowly awoke.
She was covered in darkness, but she had had no
idea where she was. The last thing she recalled was

Meredith Jessup smacking her with the shovel. Hot tears flowed down her face. This was it. This was really it for her. She was going to die and Meredith was going to get away with murder. Again. It burned her to know the woman had been walking around all this time after shooting and killing Dana's mother. And Paul? What had happened to him? Had Meredith murdered him, too? Then she'd pulled Reed into her dark deeds, making murder a family affair.

Dana took a deep breath and gasped. Wherever she was, probably at the bottom of the well Meredith had been opening, the air wouldn't last much longer. Her minutes were numbered and she wasn't ready. She'd never even given faith a chance. She'd never given God the opportunity to prove that He loved her.

No, that wasn't true. She knew the bible. She'd had nannies who had read it to her and taken her to church. They hadn't lasted long working for her mother, but they'd made an impact while she was with them. God did love. He'd proven it by giving His son to die on the cross for her. And she'd wasted the life He'd given her. She'd spent so much time feeling lonely and unloved that she hadn't even allowed herself to believe that God loved her.

And Quinn. She was certain he loved her. She'd seen it reflected in his face and felt it in his embrace. But would he live the rest of his life believing that she'd betrayed him? That would devastate him. He'd already lost so much.

She gasped for a breath. It was getting harder and

harder to breathe and she was growing sleepy, but she finally felt at peace with her life and her death.

Take care of him, Lord. I love him so much.

Quinn turned into the driveway and drove up the hill to where the house had once stood. The foundation was still there, but the place was mostly deserted. Still, he knew he was in the right place when he spotted the car Reed was known to be using by the old shed. He parked near it and saw his headlights hit on a figure on the floor. His heart wrenched. Was he already too late?

He jumped out but saw it was Reed's body, not Dana's, wrapped in plastic. He breathed a sigh of relief but knew instinctively that if Meredith was cold-hearted enough to kill her beloved nephew, Dana was in real trouble.

Moments after his arrival, the area filled with cars and deputies scanning for Dana. None of them had a stake in saving her life the way he did. He'd never told her loved her. What would he do if he never got the opportunity?

God, please keep her safe. Help me find her, Lord. I don't want to live without her.

Nothing else mattered to him now. It didn't matter that his name was all over the news channels or that his career as a covert security operator was over. His heart clenched. He'd never even gotten an opportunity to tell her he didn't believe she was the one who outed him. She still thought he was mad. Wherever she was and whatever she had been through, she'd endured it believing that he didn't trust her.

Lord, I need her to know I trust her and that I love her.

He wanted to give her everything—a home, a family, everything she'd never had growing up.

He spotted something and shined his light toward it. The iron top to the old well was out of place. He shouted to the others, "I found something."

He dropped to his knees and shoved the cover away, shining his flashlight into the hole. His heart nearly stopped when he spotted her several feet down. "Dana, can you hear me? I'm here! Hang on until I can reach you." He didn't know if she could hear him, but it made him feel better to talk to her. And maybe she could. Maybe, just maybe, his voice was comforting to her.

"I have to get down there to her," Quinn stated, but Rich grabbed his arm before he could.

"And you need to be able to get back up. I have some rope in my car. We'll lower you down."

"She's not moving." He heard the panic in his voice and he couldn't help it, but his brother remained the voice of reason.

"We have to get you both back up here, Quinn. Let us get the rope."

He finally agreed, but refused to leave the edge of the well. Rich returned with enough rope to lower him down. Quinn reached the bottom and saw Dana still hadn't moved or responded to him.

Her eyes were closed and her body was limp. He

held out his hand to touch her, terrified that he'd arrived too late.

"Dana, Dana, can you hear me?"

Her skin was still warm, but he couldn't feel any breath coming from her. He couldn't lose her now, not now, not ever. He hadn't realized the void in his life, the emptiness he'd felt at being alone. He needed her beside him as he'd never needed anyone before.

He tied the rope around her, then waited as the men above lifted her out. Then he climbed out behind her.

Quinn hit the ground and fell back away from them, watching and waiting, helpless to do anything but pray for God to spare her as Pete and another EMT rushed to help her.

Don't punish her for my mistakes, he begged. *Don't make me watch someone I care for die again.*

He couldn't take it. He just couldn't. He'd watched Tommy die, held him in his arms the same way he'd held Dana moments ago, and although his love for Tommy hadn't been romantic, their brotherly bond had been strong and his loss had shaken him. Had he not leaned on God enough and God thought he needed more suffering in order to trust Him? Why did Dana have to pay for Quinn's shortcomings? It wasn't right. It wasn't fair.

She jerked and gasped for air and Quinn's heart jerked with her. Gratitude and thankfulness flooded him at the very sound. She was back. He hadn't lost her after all. He couldn't speak as his heart overflowed with joy. He fell to his knees and praised God for His mercy.

He crawled to her side and took her hand as she drowsily looked around. When she spotted him, she gave a weak smile. He could tell it took effort, but it sent a rush of love soaring through him.

"Welcome back," he whispered, leaning down to kiss her cheek.

"What happened?"

He gave a relieved breath. "I almost lost you."

"You can't get rid of me that easily." She struggled to catch her breath.

He smiled at her efforts to make a joke then kissed her hand.

"Don't talk," he told her. They had plenty of time to tell each other everything about their lives and feelings, a new future spreading out before them.

Still, she persisted. "I have to get this out. I love you, Quinn. I love you so much." She reached up and touched his face, stroking his cheek with her hand.

Tears flooded his eyes. "I love you, too, Dana. And I'll never let you go again."

She gave him a slight, knowing smile then closed her eyes. "You'd better not."

He entered the hospital with renewed purpose, but stopped at the door that led to Dana's room. Her safety had become his utmost concern and that was a new feeling for him. He stopped and took a deep breath. Since Tommy's death, he'd closed himself off from caring or needing anyone, but she'd brought him back. He'd been in West Bend for weeks, but he hadn't felt truly at home until this moment.

He stepped in and found Dana on the bed, computer on her lap and phone at her ear. He smiled. She'd been in desperate circumstances only a few hours before and she was already back at work as if it hadn't fazed her. He knew it had, but she wouldn't let the struggle define her. It was one of the things he loved—yes, *loved*—about this incredible woman.

She spotted him in the doorway. "I'll call you back," she said into the phone, then hit the button to end her call. "What happened? What did she say?"

He hated to disappoint her. "Meredith Jessup is being tight-lipped." As predicted, she'd shut down completely after requesting a lawyer, but it seemed pretty clear to everyone involved that she'd played a part in the murders of Rene and Paul all those years ago. Mayor Jessup had even suggested his father-in-law may have assisted her or covered up for her by purchasing the Renfield property and bulldozing the house so no other evidence could be found. "Even with a lawyer on her side, she's facing serious charges. Mayor Jessup has spoken to several of his friends in the Senate who confirmed she contacted them claiming to be acting on his wishes when she asked them to phone your network. Also, he's found evidence that she paid Reed to do her bidding, including shooting Jenkins on her order."

"How is Deputy Jenkins?"

"He's doing better. He's going to make it."

He reached out and took her hand. "How are you feeling?"

"I'm going to be fine. No long-term damage. You got to me in time."

He knew from experience what it was like to not be in time to save someone he loved. He was thankful that he hadn't lost her, too. "She's going away for a long time."

A tear slipped from her eye. "She murdered my mother and tried to kill me. That woman stole everything I had, my family, my whole life. She made me believe I was unlovable."

"You're not."

He wrapped his arms around her and pulled her tightly against him and she went without hesitation. He liked that.

"Thank you for all you did, Quinn. I couldn't have done this without you. I know now why my mother died, but I had a family once, didn't I?"

"I guess you still do if you want it. Jessup was willing to do whatever it took to save you. He seems convinced you're his daughter." She'd lost so much but she'd found family, too. "What will you do now? Go back to the show?"

"Yes. I found my answers, but there are a lot of families out there that haven't gotten theirs. I feel like it's my duty to help them."

"I like that."

She looked up at him and he saw the question in her face. "What about you? What will you do now that you can't go back to contract work?"

Her voice still held a tinge of guilt and he wanted to quickly dispel that. He took her hand. "Dana, I don't blame you for what happened. I know you wouldn't purposefully do anything to hurt me."

"I wouldn't, but it seems I did anyway. I asked my friend Tracy to look in to some things and she found you instead. I'm so sorry, Quinn. I want you to trust me."

"I do trust you, Dana. I trust you more than any other person in my life. To answer your original question, I've been fielding calls from all kinds of government entities, senators, representatives from every committee there is. And Rizzo and I were talking with some of the other guys about writing a book about our experience. People need to know what happened that night and how their government failed to act. I guess I'll be traveling the country for a while."

She smiled. "Me, too."

He pulled her into his arms and kissed her long and hard. "How about, when I'm done with my traveling and you're done with yours, we meet back here."

"I'd like that, but are you sure that's what you want?"

"I don't know what's going to happen in my life over the next year, Dana. I don't know what's going to happen with my career or how many panels and interviews I'll have to give. All I do know is that when it's all said and done, I want to come back home and I want you here with me."

A radiant smile spread across her face. "You do?"

"Absolutely. You came searching for family. Well,

you gained more than you bargained for in West Bend. I always want you to think of this place as your home. How about we meet back here six months from today? I'll bring a preacher and we'll make you an official member of the Dawson family and an official resident of West Bend?"

Her eyes were sparkling as she wrapped her arms around his neck. "I would love that," she whispered. "In case you can't find me, I'll be the one dressed in white."

He grinned. "Don't you worry. I'll find you."

"You always do."

She leaned into his chest. As he held her, he vowed she would never be alone again.

* * * * *

Don't miss these
Rangers Under Fire
books by Virginia Vaughan:

Yuletide Abduction
Reunion Mission
Ranch Refuge
Mistletoe Reunion Threat
Mission Undercover
Mission: Memory Recall

Available now from Love Inspired Suspense!

Find more great reads at www.LoveInspired.com

Dear Reader,

Is there anything more fun than finding a new series to delve into? It's the same for writers!

I'm so thankful to have the opportunity to start this new series, Covert Operatives, with Quinn and Dana's story. These were two such independent characters that at times they were difficult for even me to understand. But they both needed the same thing we all do—love and family. Coming from a rather large family myself, I sometimes wish I had the freedom to pick up and go and do my own thing without having to worry about family obligations, but when I delve into a story like this one and remember there are so many people out there like Dana—possibly even some of my readers—who are searching for the very thing I often take for granted, I'm humbled and thankful.

I hope you enjoyed this story and will continue with me on this journey into this new series.

I love hearing from my readers! You can connect with me online through my website virginiavaughan-online.com and at facebook.com/ginvaughanbooks.

Sincerely,
Virginia Vaughan

OCT   2018